About the Author

Growing up female in the 1950s was peculiar. We were kept like children till sixteen when we were given nylon stockings to wear and supposed to change instantly into adults.

When my youngest sister read this story she sent me an abrupt postcard. 'Thanks for book. Read it. Can't say I approve.' The other sisters also simmered. They felt I had transformed our shared past into romantic fiction.

If there's one truthful part, it's the title. Our mother wouldn't give us any information about sex and reproduction, even though we often asked. Instead, she told us, 'Never ever forget that love is stronger than mountains.'

Half a century on and we all know now that she was absolutely right.

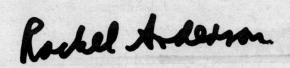

Look out for other titles in the Moving Times trilogy

Grandmother's Footsteps
Bloom of Youth

Also by Rachel Anderson

Blackthorn, Whitethorn
The Flight of the Emu
Pizza on Saturday
Red Moon

Other titles published by Hodder Children's Books

The Glittering Eye
Cherry Heaven
The Diary of Pelly D
L.J. Adlington

The Carbon Diaries 2015
Saci Lloyd

Stronger than Mountains

RACHEL ANDERSON

Hodder
Children's
Books

A division of Hachette Children's Books

A Catalogue record for this book is available
from the British Library

ISBN 978 0 340 98160 3

Typeset in Bembo by Avon DataSet Ltd,
Bidford-on-Avon, Warwickshire

Printed and bound in Great Britain by
CPI Bookmarque, Croydon

The paper and board used in this paperback by Hodder
Children's Books are natural recyclable products made from
wood grown in sustainable forests. The manufacturing
processes conform to the environmental regulations of
the country of origin.

Hodder Children's Books
a division of Hachette Children's Books
338 Euston Road, London NW1 3BH
An Hachette UK company
www.hachette.co.uk

Contents

THOSE WERE THE DAYS, MY LOVE

ONCE UPON A TIME

ONE

God Bless This Grinning Bride

Once upon a time, there lived a poor, yet talented and unusually vivacious young widow. Her deceased husband had left her with five children, some unpaid bills, and not much else. She fed, sheltered and reared her brood as best she could. This was rarely in any conventional manner since she was constantly thinking up bizarre methods of childcare, based on the principle of saving money while having fun.

The widow had been baptised with the name 'Veritas'.

'What a beastly burden to carry through life!' said her best friend Denise.

It was not even a proper Christian name, more a bit of old Latin, *veritas* providing the root for a range of useful everyday words: very, veriest, verify, verisimilitude, veritable.

It was a curious name for a person who rarely kept to the truth. Long before she became widowed, Veritas had been exaggerating the facts, stretching the imagination, embroidering the truth, doctoring the evidence.

As well she should, for her wild distortions and fictions

became the youth pageants by which means she supported her hungry semi-orphans.

I knew the truth of this, for the well-known writer and wireless personality was my very own mother. I had lived with her long enough to understand and accept that the enthusiastic falsehoods, fabrications, fibs, porkies, and whoppers were her stock-in-trade.

However, there was one essential truth-hood which she stuck to throughout the years she spent trying to rear me and my four siblings. And it was this:

'Always remember, Ruth, that love is stronger than mountains.'

'Yes, Mum.'

She repeated it so often that I began to believe it was a quotation from the Scriptures.

'Thtwonger fan *what*?' asked Blanche, my second-to-youngest sister, with interest. She was interested in anything I did. I should have been proud. I was not. I was irritated. 'Don't pick up fag ends, Blanchie,' I told her sharply.

'Than mountains,' said Veritas firmly.

'What is?' my very youngest sister, Felicity, wanted to know. She too liked to pick up the fag-end of any conversation which wasn't intended for her ears.

'Love is,' Veritas repeated. 'Which is why, as I've told Ruth many times, she and Mary must be very, very careful now they're growing up.'

Mary was the eldest, and wisest, of the five of us.

'Careful about what?' asked little Felicity, who was so

young she'd only just started primary school, so young that she earnestly believed those soppy old ladies who told her that her dead daddy was looking down on her from heaven to check she was still being a good little girl.

'You'll know about it when you're older, Felicity,' I said, which was what people had told me when I was her age. Besides, I didn't think it was up to an elder sister to have to explain the facts of life to a five-year-old when she hardly knew them herself. That was a mother's job, if indeed it was the facts of life Veritas was referring to when she spoke of the strength of love. Or was it merely a fanciful attempt to prevent Mary and me from falling into evil and enjoyable ways with the three boys in winklepicker boots we'd just met in the Black and White Moo-Cow Milk Bar?

However, at that moment, Veritas was in no position to explain anything, true or otherwise, to any of her daughters. She had a livelihood to earn. She hurried back to her typewriter to finish writing her latest children's pageant which was based on a whole load of historical exaggerations about the Royal Family.

Eventually, it would earn enough money to pay another bill in the pile waiting at the other end of the table.

Family life was dominated by the need to pay the bills with the red FINAL DEMAND warning on them. The electricity hadn't yet been cut off though the general grocer often came to the door to say he wouldn't deliver another order till the last three accounts had been settled. It took Mary a few moments of quiet persuasion, mostly by putting her head on one side and looking sadly at her bare feet, to convince Mr Bradsack that his bills were definitely at the top of the pile.

Veritas may not have been talented at handling truth or money but she was spot-on when it came to the strength of the mountains. I had barely become a grown-up when true love sought me out and held me in its powerful grip.

'But, Ruthie, how can you be sure,' Felicity asked with solemn interest, 'that it's *true* love and not the other kind?'

'What other kind?'

'The cruel faithless kind?'

What did a seven-year-old know of faithless love?

'I can't be sure,' I said. I knew only that, exactly as Veritas had forewarned, this love thing was far stronger than any other emotion I'd experienced, stronger even than the surge of triumph I felt when I was offered my best-ever job in a newspaper office.

And it was because of the power of love that, one May morning, I handed in my notice to the editor. And one bright June afternoon two weeks later, I found myself shuffling down the narrow concrete stairway outside the flat above a lock-up garage where Veritas, my siblings and I lived. I was on my way to a church at the top of a hill to marry a young man I was crazy about, yet hardly knew.

I was wearing a billowing white garment more like a shower curtain than a bridal gown, and a pair of borrowed white sling-backs with long pointy toes. They were a size and a half too large. They may have fitted Mary last summer;

they certainly didn't fit me this summer.

Mary went down to the street to hail a taxi. This was an absurd extravagance. It would cost half a day's wages. We never took taxis anywhere.

'Why don't we walk?' I said.

'This is the most important day of your life,' Mary said sternly. 'You've got to remember it for ever. And anyway, you'd never make it in those shoes.'

A taxi pulled over. Mary lifted her baby's carrycot in. I scrambled in after.

'Day out, is it, girls?' the driver asked over his shoulder.

Wasn't it obvious we were on our way to a wedding? I thought till, catching sight of my reflection, I realised he might easily have thought we were off to a fancy dress parade.

Our taxi was soon stuck in a jam near the tube station.

'Come on, come on,' I muttered through gritted teeth. 'If we don't get a move on, we'll miss it.'

Mary calmed me down. 'If he's any good, he'll wait,' she said.

We reached the church at twenty-five to three. I could see people standing around outside in relaxed party mood. We hadn't missed it. But it was a mild summer's afternoon. Nobody except for me seemed to want to go inside.

Veritas, wearing a strange hat she'd made out of some fly-screen netting, and which now looked like a stiff overcooked meringue dumped on her head, was already there. Also my scary uncles, Falcon, Merlin, Kestrel, and the

Reverend Guillemot who was a vicar. He'd been named after a sea bird. In middle age he was finally beginning to look like one, waddling about outside his church as though on webbed feet.

He'd always known how hard up his sister Veritas was. 'So I imagine any chaps your daughters decide to marry will be hard up too,' he'd observed accurately. He'd offered to conduct my marriage, waiving the usual three-guinea fee.

There were people outside the church I didn't recognise. They must be from my Beloved's family.

And where was *he*?

My heart sank like a broken lift down to the over-sized sling-backs. What if he'd decided to call it off?

'Of *course* he's here,' Mary said soothingly. 'He wouldn't let you down. Not if he really loves you. And he does, doesn't he?'

I wasn't sure. I knew I loved him. I'd have to see his kind, trustworthy smile to be reassured of his feelings towards me.

'Strong as mountains,' I said firmly and stepped from the taxi. Mary handed out the carrycot while she looked for her purse to pay the driver.

Veritas was standing near some gravestones. She caught sight of our cheerful arrival. She began to flap her hands excitedly as though trying to blow out a small fire. She came hurrying down the path towards us.

'Go away!' she panted, flapping more frantically. 'Mary!

Get her back in the taxi. Quickly, before anybody sees.'

'What's wrong?' Mary asked calmly.

'You're early. No bride worth anything arrives ahead of time. And get that baby out of sight!'

Mary snatched her baby from the carrycot and held her protectively.

I said, 'What d'you mean, calling Stella "*that* baby"? She's your own treasured grandchild.'

'I know she is,' said Veritas. 'And she looks gorgeous. But whatever will people think, seeing the bride arriving *with* a baby? They'll think it's yours.'

Only the evening before, she'd said that the dress I'd made out of pillow-case cotton was too voluminous.

'Everyone'll think you're eight months gone.'

I could hardly have a three-month-old baby *and* be in an advanced state of pregnancy. Besides, I didn't care what anybody thought, apart from the Beloved.

I said, 'And everybody knows the proverb that bringing a baby to a wedding bestows good fortune on the couple.'

'Not at this wedding it doesn't.'

I said, 'It's an ancient Chinese saying. I'm surprised you've never heard it before.'

'*Please*, Ruthie,' Veritas pleaded. 'Nobody's ready for you yet.'

'But *I'm* ready. I *want* to get married. I do. I do. I do. And I'm sure Harry's ready.' I tried to imagine him alone in the cool dark church, waiting expectantly.

Veritas said, 'I'm not at all sure he's arrived yet.' I hoped she was lying. 'So off you go.'

Mary whispered into my ear. 'Of course he'll be there. But let's do as she says if it makes her happy. It is her big day after all.'

'Hers? I thought you said it was mine.'

'More hers,' said Mary, pushing me back into the taxi.

Veritas looked relieved. She adjusted her fly-net hat. 'There's my good girls. Go for a short spin and come back later.'

'How much later?' I asked through the open window. It was twenty to three. Veritas didn't specify. She handed the driver half a crown. 'Would you kindly take my daughters and granddaughter up to the park and back?'

'Righto, lady,' said the cabbie and drove at funeral pace towards the park gates. He circled the pond in the park. We watched children sailing toy boats and flying their poster-colour kites, holding balloons, eating vanilla and strawberry ices which melted in the hot sun and dribbled down their elbows in pastel stripes.

I said, 'This is my last-ever sight as a spinster of ordinary people doing ordinary Saturday things.'

The driver took us twice round the pond. I was sure I could hear a clock strike three. I grew impatient with ordinary people doing ordinary things.

'It *must* be time by now!'

'No. Five to three,' said Mary. She got the taxi to stop beside the ice-cream seller's tricycle. She hopped out and bought three ice-cream wafers: one for me, one for her, one for the taxi-driver.

'Ooh ta, love,' he said. He drove slowly back to the church. We arrived at three minutes past three. It seemed to me to be far too late but was obviously about right. I could see the guests sauntering casually, almost reluctantly, in through the doors.

Mary tried to pay the driver but he was so pleased with his ice-cream wafer that, like Uncle Guillemot, he waived any fee.

'God bless, duckie,' he said. 'And good luck!'

'Thanks.' I hoped there might be another ancient proverb about getting a free ride out of a London cabbie on your wedding day bringing a bride eternal joy.

TWO

Who Gives This Woman?

I slip-slopped across the churchyard as briskly as I could in the dangerously large sling-backs. Mary followed with the carrycot. Baby Stella was gurgling contentedly, waving her tiny hands at the church spire.

She was so dainty, so alive, so perfectly her parents' darling. And she was the reason I was getting married. The moment I'd seen her at one day old in Mary's arms, I'd known I didn't just want the Beloved. I wanted his babies too.

Mary paused to pick a sprig of white jasmine from where it was growing vigorously over a tilting headstone. She tucked it into my hand.

'Here, Ruthie. Hold this, like a bouquet. I told Mum I'd make you one. Sorry. Didn't have time.'

The jasmine smelled as sweet as warm honey. It reminded me of a boy I'd met in Greece. Outside an isolated Orthodox chapel perched on a rocky hill looking out over the blue Aegean sea, he'd picked me whole armfuls of jasmine. There and then, we'd decided to marry. The ancient priest was a soppy romantic who seemed prepared to do it for us. In the nick of time, I realised the boy and I were in love with Greek history rather than with each other.

All that was last year, back in the past. I was on to my new life now.

Veritas, in her flat meringue hat, was on the church steps hustling my brother, my two younger sisters (who looked unusually clean), and a third little girl with clumpy brown school sandals peeking out beneath the hem of the blue bridesmaid's dress. She looked terribly shy, yet faintly familiar. Was she some long-lost cousin I'd forgotten we had?

I grinned encouragingly but she was busy trying to keep her sensible Clark's footwear out of sight. Her eyes and nose were a bit like the Beloved's. Yes, she must be his kid sister. Within the hour, she'd be my sister too. I'd share the same surname and I'd be a 'Mrs'.

'Well *done*, girls!' Veritas congratulated Mary and me as though we'd achieved something greater than fiddling away fourteen minutes eating ice-cream. 'You've timed it *exactly* right!'

I peered round her to catch a reassuring glimpse of the Beloved.

'It's an absurd out-dated superstition,' I muttered, 'not letting people see each other until they meet at the altar. I know *grandfather* wouldn't have approved. And probably not *father* either.'

I'd managed to stop missing my father every second of

every hour ages ago. But on this significant day, there came a stabbing recurrence of that old despair. If only he were here now, to see me, all grown up. If only he'd been able to meet the gentle man waiting for me. If only my man could have met him. Surely they would have had much in common.

An elderly couple came scurrying towards the church, desperate to slip in unobtrusively ahead of us.

'We're late! We're late!' twitched the old fellow, like the white rabbit in *Alice in Wonderland*. Veritas greeted them with kisses which prompted them to kiss me too. I hadn't a clue who they were.

'Green pottery egg cups,' Mary whispered in my ear.

'What?'

'Old acquaintances.'

'Not mine,' I said.

'No, Mum's. They sent you green egg cups.'

'Oh.' Dimly, I recalled the arrival of a wedding present, and my own confusion as to why I might need to start married life with egg cups for six when I hadn't even got a marital home sorted out. But I'd written a courteous thank-you note, and promptly given the egg-cups to Mary to use for mixing her oil paints.

I should have felt grateful. I just felt annoyed. Why did any of these unknown people from our mother's past have to be here in their dark morning suits and gaudy petalled hats? Surely this event was a matter between me and the man of my dreams (with the possible inclusion of the

Almighty, since, according to Uncle Guillemot, the marriage would be conducted in the sight of God)?

When my father married Veritas during the London blitz, there'd been none of this fuss. No one else had been present except the vicar and an unknown GI soldier they'd lured out of the cocktail bar at the Ritz Hotel to be their witness.

'We only did it that way,' Veritas used to say, 'because of the bombing. You had to be quick. You never knew what might happen next. We'd have preferred it like this.'

I didn't believe her. Her hasty marriage, at twenty-four hours' notice, backed by the whine of air-raid sirens, illuminated by searchlights raking the skies, had been truly romantic.

Inside the church, I could see the silhouette of Uncle Guillemot bobbing towards me like a big white bird. The long surplice over the black cassock was as lacking in style as my own bunchy dress. He beamed a smile of holy encouragement.

'Come along now, Ruthie,' Veritas hissed instructions. 'Take Alfred George's arm nicely.'

I remembered the numerous days when I'd had to hold my brother's arm to drag him, kicking and screaming, down the road to school.

Now, at fourteen, he was as tall as a man, and was dressed as a man in our father's tailcoat and striped trousers, with our father's top hat under his arm. But no way could I consider him as a man. Besides, we weren't on speaking terms. Two days ago, he'd sneaked my typewriter down to the pawnbroker's shop and pawned it for five pounds.

'It's worth far more than that,' I'd said. 'And I need it. It's the tool of my trade.'

'You won't be earning your living while you're away on honeymoon.'

'So where's the five quid then?'

'I needed some cash rather urgently.'

'What for?'

He paused, then said so quickly I knew he was lying, 'To buy you a present.'

'Don't be daft. I've got far too many presents as it is.' People I'd never heard of were sending me things like egg cup sets, not because they knew me, but because they felt so relieved that poor widowed Veritas was managing to get rid of another of her wretched daughters.

'You can get it back,' Alfred George assured me. 'Honest Injun.'

His honesty was as reliable as our mother's, so I'd resolved not to speak to him till the typewriter was returned intact.

Here in the church, he didn't seem any more keen to have me clutching on to him than I was to clutch.

'Do I have to hold on to him?' I asked Veritas.

'Yes. You know he's supposed to be *giving you away*.'

It was her idea that Alfred George should take the important role of father of the bride who escorts his daughter up the aisle and hands her over into the care of the groom. But since the pawnshop business, no way would I trust my brother, a mere schoolboy, to do anything as responsible as hand something over to the person it was intended for.

'I don't *need* giving away,' I muttered. We'd been through all this before. Had we got to have it out again? 'Couldn't we just walk along side by side, like normal people?'

'No. You've got to do this thing properly. You know it's what Father would have wanted.' She always said that about anything *she* wanted.

Alfred George and I jostled and struggled in the entrance while the three bridesmaids grew restless behind us. Then the organ music started, very loud, very thrilling. All heads turned to stare, a sea of expectant faces and bobbing hats.

'Oh, do come *on*, Ruth, and let's just get it *over with*!' said Alfred George, as though it was some disagreeable task rather than the big crossroads of my life. 'Let's make up, just for the next hour. If you can't bear to hold my arm like she says, I'll hold *yours*. OK?'

So I abandoned the struggle for sibling supremacy. He was right. This was no place or time to re-enact all our childish tiffs. Reluctantly I let him take my arm.

'And one more thing, Ruth,' Veritas whispered. She was full of advice today. I supposed she thought it was her last chance. In fact, I supposed wrong. 'Remember not to smile till it's over.'

'But I'm happy, Mum.' Or I will be soon.

'Yes, I know, and it's all really lovely. But you're looking far too eager. It's not dignified in a bride.'

Alfred George hooked his arm through mine so that,

though he appeared to be tenderly guiding me to my destiny, neither of us actually had to touch. We set off with the little girls prancing merrily along behind. Our procession seemed to take forever. I wished Veritas hadn't insisted on Uncle Guillemot's church which had such a long nave. And the sling-backs really were most uncomfortable. And the jasmine sprig was wilting in my hot hand.

'By the way, there's something else,' Alfred George whispered. 'It wasn't really to buy you a present.'

'What was it for then?' I whispered back.

'To run away to get a job in the country.'

'Don't be daft. It's illegal. You've got to stay at school.'

'No I haven't. They expelled me on Wednesday.'

Why did he have to tell me today? Perhaps it was just as well the church was so long. It gave us a few seconds more.

'You idiot! What on earth for?'

'Tell you later.'

'No.' He must tell me now. By this evening, I wouldn't be around any more. We reached the chancel steps, the end of our walk. I whispered fiercely, 'Well, you're absolutely not to run anywhere without telling Mum where you're going. She'd be worried sick. And so would I.'

He nodded. 'OK. I promise.'

I wondered if he'd keep his promise.

'By the way,' he added, 'when you need your typewriter back, the pawnbroker's ticket's in the breadbin.'

With that, Alfred George stepped aside into the shadows

and the Beloved stepped into the limelight beside me. Uncle Guillemot asked in a loud voice if anybody could show any just cause why we shouldn't be lawfully joined together and if so, he was to speak.

'Or else hereafter forever hold his peace.'

Luckily nobody could think of any objections. That was probably because most of the congregation, being pre-war pals of Veritas, didn't know me from Eve, nor my Beloved from Adam.

I took a quick sideways peek to make sure it was him and that he and his pal, the best man, hadn't swapped places as a jolly undergraduate jape. I'd known the best man, also called Harry, since I was eight. He'd introduced me to his best university pal, also Harry. And as though a thunderbolt from heaven had sought us out, we were struck by love, then unstruck. Then struck again.

Whew. It was OK. The chosen Harry stood beside me. His expression was so serious, his eyes so blue and twinkling, his hair so bright and wavy, the back of his neck so smooth and vulnerable, sliding down into the starched white collar of his wedding shirt, his ears so tender and delicious.

Lovely Harry, my almost-husband, gave an almost imperceptible nod of recognition. I tried not to grin with delight.

Uncle Guillemot got on with it at a cracking good pace. Almost before I knew it, we'd got to the bit where the Beloved said he would, 'Take Ruth to my wedded wife, to have and to hold from this day forward, for better for worse, for richer for poorer, in sickness and in health, to love and to cherish till death us do part.'

As he said the words, I was struck by another thunderbolt. This time, it was the thought that death, like love, was every bit as strong as mountains and could arrive at any moment. It might come and seek me out this very day. Even if it waited till next week, Harry and I still wouldn't have enough time to get to know one another properly. I certainly wouldn't have time to tell him all the things I wanted to. Not that I intended to tell him *everything* about my past. A few things were best left unsaid, such as that boy I didn't marry in Greece. In fact, I hadn't even mentioned him in my private journal.

If I died, Harry would have to rely on his new, untrustworthy mother-in-law for the story of his deceased bride's life.

That would be bad enough. But here was the disastrous bit: Veritas would try to tell Harry a whole load of fanciful exaggerations about events that had never happened. And because Harry had studied Latin and knew that her name meant 'truth', he'd believe her. It was an awesome thought.

I had to make sure it didn't happen. So I gabbled speedily through the vows, as instructed by Uncle Guillemot, promising to take Harry to be my wedded husband, to love him till death parted us, to plight him my troth. Then, under my breath, I plighted the other troth which was that I would set down everything more or less as it had been (except for those bits I was intending to leave out), to convey to him the reality of that girlhood which had been deeply unhappy yet, simultaneously, profoundly secure. Then, should our magnificent marriage end prematurely due to my early demise, he'd at least know who I had been, or who I wanted him to think I had been.

I felt a weight off my mind. I couldn't interfere with the dominion of death. But I could set the record straight, in the way that I wanted it to be set, concerning my own past.

However, as a daughter of Veritas, and as a busy writer of personal journals in my youth, I knew truth to be a variable and elusive objective. What you left out was often as significant as what you put in. Moreover, before any autobiographies could be written, there was the more urgent matter of my brother's troubles to be investigated.

By the time Harry and I came swinging joyfully down the aisle, my arm cosily tucked into his, his sweet hand holding mine, there was no sign of Alfred George anywhere. The surrogate father of the bride had long since left to seek his fortune and to escape his creditors, namely me.

IN DAYS OF YORE

THREE

Baby Blue Eyes

Veritas and my father were posh but poor. They lived and looked grander than they should have. They sent his shirts and collars to the laundry to be returned stiffly starched, and wrapped in delicate tissue, yet our sheets were grey, with rips. We ate with Georgian silver cutlery but the meal was toast and dripping. The window-cleaner saw to the front of the house but not the back. Veritas was gloved and hatted when she went out. Indoors, she wore our father's dressing-gown.

'It's pure silk,' she said proudly. 'He had it made for him in Jermyn Street.'

That must have been centuries back when he was still a spry man-about-town. Now the paisley silk was worn as thin as the sheets.

For years, I had to sleep in a baby's drop-side cot because they couldn't afford to buy another bed. My baby brother slept in a potato basket. Veritas tied pretty blue satin ribbons round the edge and called it the *bercelonette*.

'That's French for a rocking cradle,' she said.

It still looked like a vegetable-picker's basket to me.

'Which is a sight more than he deserves,' said Mary who'd not wanted this gift of a brother in the first place.

'Isn't she getting a bit big for that drop-side cot by now?' my mother's interfering sister Speranza asked. 'She'll grow up all twisted.'

'It's an extra-long cot,' said Veritas breezily. 'And she's an extra-small girl for her age. So there's still plenty of room.'

'I didn't mean her spine would be twisted. I meant her outlook will be twisted,' said Aunt Speranza.

'No, Ruthie loves her nice comfy cot,' insisted Veritas with enthusiasm. 'Don't you, darling?'

I was a dutiful daughter. It never occurred to me that I should have a whole bed of my own.

I nodded. The cot was duck-egg blue, with transfers of bunnies and dappled leaping Bambis. But the rabbits had faded to the same dun colour as Bambi, for the cot wasn't new. Veritas had looted it from a bomb-site when Mary was born.

Looting was a shootable offence. Veritas hadn't been caught otherwise I'd not have had a chance to exist.

There were brownish scorch marks on the paintwork. One of my scary uncles, Kestrel, named after a meat-eating bird of prey, told me it was caused by an incendiary bomb and I should claim reparation money from the Ministry of Defence. He was probably making it up in the same way that his sister made things up. And he obviously didn't know that his sister had looted it.

One side of the cot was jammed in the lowered position. I was free to climb out when I pleased. Uncle Kestrel, who'd spent the war years beneath the Atlantic Ocean in a submarine, called it 'Ruth's escape hatch'.

The rest of the tall thin house was so crowded out with lodgers, students, uncles on leave from the navy, the army or the Church training college, that it was an advantage to have a territorial space, however small, that was entirely one's own. I could read peacefully without being tripped over.

'So it's not *really* a cot at all,' said Veritas, proving her facility at stretching the truth to accommodate her own viewpoint. 'It's more of a small bed with a fence on three sides.'

At school, they moved me up to a higher class. We did multiplications and long divisions and were considered old enough to be punished with a swift swish of the cane for lazy thinking or slack behaviour. Yet at home I continued to sleep in a baby's cot.

I knew it wasn't normal.

Bambi had a bed of ferns in a forest. Snow White had a glass coffin. Other people at school had beds, even when they had to share them with all their brothers. My elder sister Mary had a bed.

'That's because she's got long legs,' said Veritas. 'She's going to be very tall like your father.'

'Stumpy legs,' Mary called me.

Some evenings, to prove I didn't mind the cot or the legs, I invited her into the burn-marked cot. We sat, scrumpled up, one at each end and I read aloud to her. I liked reading more than I liked going to school and facing the threat of the swishy cane for wrong sums.

I became ill with pains in my legs as though the bones had turned into thorny brambles. I couldn't climb over the lowered side of the cot. I couldn't walk downstairs. I lay and whimpered.

Mary didn't call me 'stumpy legs' any more.

'Here's our friendly family doctor,' said Veritas, fibbing as usual, as she showed a dour stranger into the bedroom. He examined my legs with cold hands.

I was taken to hospital for further examination. Nobody explained what might be wrong but I heard them muttering the names of Veritas's favourite fears – infantile paralysis, rheumatic fever, juvenile arthritis, tuberculosis.

I just wanted my legs to stop hurting.

Veritas and I were sent home. She said, 'You're to have complete bed-rest for the rest of the term. Won't that be fun!'

How could I have bed-rest when I hadn't got a bed?

My arithmetic books were sent from school to join me in the cot. Veritas's moth-eaten fur coat, which she was keeping in case she and our father ever got invited to a garden party at Buckingham Palace, also joined me as an extra blanket. It was like having to share the cramped cot with an old dead bear.

Veritas said, 'It's mink, darling. Not bear. Nobody wears bear any more.'

They couldn't afford to buy new blankets for us. Or clothes. But friends sent their cast-offs.

'Look, dear sweet Véronique has given you a pair of her old practice leggings to keep your legs snug and warm,' said Veritas. 'Isn't that exciting, to have a real dancer's leggings?'

Véronique was a ballerina from our father's glamorous past. Her pass-on tights were scratchy wool. They were a sicky mustard-yellow. They were footless. My naked feet stuck out from the end.

'*Please* don't make me wear them,' I begged. 'People will laugh.'

But Veritas insisted. 'You have to be kept warm. It's a great honour to be wearing a famous star's leggings.'

Nobody laughed, not even Mary. She said, 'Poor you,' and drew faces on my toenails to cheer me up.

I wasn't cheered. I became restless and morose. Was I doomed to stay trapped in a drop-side cot doing sums for ever?

'You're ruining my life,' I grumbled. It was lonely, even with the dead creature which was not a bear. Would I be lonely for the rest of my life?

Veritas had an idea. She often had ideas. It was calmer when she didn't.

'I know what we'll do, Ruthie,' she said, clapping her hands with delight at her innovation. 'We'll move you downstairs. You can have my trunk! It'll make a wonderful bed for you. What fun!'

Her trunk was a flat-topped storage chest. Nobody had ever slept on it before.

'So it's a very special privilege,' Veritas said with such an encouraging smile that I knew it was no such thing. The truth of the matter was that the baby had outgrown the ribbon-trimmed potato basket. It was his turn for the looted cot.

Inside the trunk were personal things which Veritas had managed to keep with her throughout the war, even when she was bombed out. PRIVATE was stencilled on the lid. The word was a challenge. Mary and I had sifted through the contents many times, usually when Veritas and our father were out at The Drayman's Arms which was, so Veritas said, the only place where they could get any time to themselves.

In the trunk she kept a black hat decorated with a bunch of artificial cherries. Mary claimed our mother had been wearing it the first time she met our father.

'Why did she wear pretend cherries on her head?'

'I expect she thought it was smart,' Mary said. 'Probably even a bit fast, specially for a parson's daughter.'

'Fast?' I said.

'You know, alluring. Provocative. That's how she managed to attract his attention.'

The black hat was now crushed though the bright cherries still looked good enough to eat.

'That's what being provocative's all about,' Mary said knowingly.

Since Veritas had succeeded in catching our father, why, I wondered, would she want to hang on to the hat?

Mary said, 'Maybe it's in case she ever gets invited to a garden party at Buckingham Palace.'

'But she doesn't know the King,' I said.

'No, but one day she might do something really heroic, like Uncle Falcon rescuing that pilot from a burning plane. Then she'd get invited.'

Also in the trunk were twenty-four silver-plated fruit forks which Veritas had retrieved from the knife drawer in the hope they might be worth pawning, and two dozen notebooks filled with her unreadable scrawl. These, had I known it, were the most valuable treasure our family possessed. They would provide a future income for all of us.

There was no space for the trunk upstairs, so I and my painful mustard-yellow legs and my arithmetic books were helped downstairs.

'It'll be so much more interesting for you here in the drawing room, won't it, Ruthie?' said Veritas. 'You'll be at the epicentre of events. You'll get to see everything that's going on.'

Thus it was that I came to witness far more than I wanted, something more painful than arthritic limbs or

canings for wrong sums. It was an event which made me
fear for the foundations of family life.

FOUR

Turbulent Night

Veritas only called it a drawing room to make it sound more elegant. It was a hybrid through-space. A pram, a piano and bicycles lived there. It was also her writing room. It was a short cut from the front door to the back yard. It was where the washing was draped in wet weather. Now it was also my new bedroom or, rather, my trunkroom.

'You won't be lonely any more!' said Veritas. 'Not with so much jolly come-and-go!'

I could watch and listen as Veritas pounded away at the keys of her Imperial typewriter. And where she was, so was everybody else:

    – the milkman wanting to be paid

    – ditto the dusty-faced coalman

    – Susie, the visitor from France, wondering what to do about my baby brother, with whom she shared a room, who was yelling himself red in the face

    – the student lodgers coming to pay their two guineas a week or, more often, to say, 'Ever so sorry, Mrs Vee, can't manage it this week. Will next week do?'

– Mary coming home from school and weeping on the floor over her homework.

That was during the day. Come the night all bustling ceased.

'You'll be quite safe, Ruthie,' Veritas said as she tucked me up under her old fur. 'There's nice Mr and Mrs Riggs just underneath you and all of us upstairs.'

Downstairs on a trunk, alone with the shadows of the plane trees dancing spooky foxtrots on the walls, was a dismal place to be.

Two of the lodgers, an unemployed one-armed ex-serviceman and his wife, lived like troglodytes in the basement. But they were so far below, they might have been buried deep in a coalmine for all the companionship they provided. The rest of the inhabitants were so far above that they might as well have been snoozing on a cloud in heaven. Even Mrs Riggs's cat wouldn't stay with me for it distrusted the smell of the dead not-bear.

As bravely as Uncle Falcon and the flaming Spitfire, I endured the hours of loneliness. Then, late one windy night, I was woken by two harsh voices. Adult figures were arguing in the hallway. I buried my head under the fur but the anger still reached me.

They were interrupted by the timid turning of a latchkey in the front door. An art student returning late. The couple stepped back into the darkened room where I lay, to be out of sight of the student. Had they forgotten I was on the trunk and supposed to be having complete rest? The student tiptoed softly upstairs. They continued their fearsome row.

Could this really be my devoted parents, known to all for their mutual adoration? I listened. I quivered. Their discord was more terrifying than any number of screaming sirens. How could they do this? They'd survived the terrible years of raids and evacuations, of separations and threats of Nazi invasion. Now it sounded as though they were about to kill each other.

It was about money. They hadn't enough. One of them had spent what they once had. Now they hadn't any. Each blamed the other for their lack.

'All right then, go!' she said. 'If that's what you want! You go and find a better way to live. Back with your fabulous friends.'

'*I* don't want to go. *You* said you want me to go.'

'Too late for that! I'm the one's who's leaving! And don't you count on me coming back!'

If she left, who would feed the baby? Who would plait my hair? Our family would be destroyed.

'Don't be a foolish old cow, my darling. It's after midnight. Let's sleep on it and talk about it again in the morning.'

'Don't you darling me!'

'Where will you go? Off to Ruth as usual!'

'Don't bring my mother into this. And no, I'm not! I'm going somewhere you'll never find me.'

I heard the front door open and close. What could she do in the middle of a windy night with no coat? She hadn't even bothered to retrieve her treasures from inside the trunk. If only she had, she'd have seen me. She'd have remembered she couldn't abandon us.

I heard my father start wearily for the stairs.

'Father!' I called out. 'Don't let her go! Fetch her back!'

He sauntered back into the room, too casually for a man whose wife had just left him. He stroked the top of my head. 'I say, old thing, don't weep now. She'll return in her own good time.'

How could he be certain?

'My affection for your dear mother is as solid as rock,' he said. 'I believe the feeling is reciprocated.'

I clung to his hand. He switched on the light. Wasting electricity! That certainly wasn't going to help solve the family's money troubles. He looked so tired.

'Listen, old girl, if you can't sleep, you might like this.' Tucked under his arm was his copy of *The Times*, neatly folded. He handed it to me, said goodnight, and went upstairs.

Nobody had ever offered me such adult reading matter. I struggled with the large unwieldy pages which ripped in my hands as easily as worn bed-sheets. I looked at the headlines.

CLOTH PRICES UP, I READ. UTILITY CORSETS TO BE DEARER.

Then, MINE SPOTTED IN THE CHANNEL. EXPLODED BY DESTROYER.

And, DOUBLE PETROL RATION FOR SUMMER. I knew that

was good news, even if you didn't own a car and couldn't benefit.

I read BLACK MARKET THRIVES! Customs officials had broken up the biggest nylon stocking smuggling ring in Britain, seizing thousands of pairs hidden in an ocean liner.

The war, during which my parents had met and fallen in love, was long over but its effects were lingering on.

I tried to do the crossword puzzle which was printed on the back page of *The Times*. But the clues were difficult and I didn't have a pencil. So I lay awake mourning the loss of my mother, yearning for the sound of her key scrabbling at the front door.

Her leaving was my fault. If I'd been more grateful for my meagre lot, they wouldn't have fought. If I'd kept quiet about my legs, she wouldn't have had to waste time at the hospital. She'd have spent time finishing her pageant. She'd have earned money. Another bill would have been paid.

Next morning, I was woken by familiar crashing and thumping from the kitchen. Porridge was being cooked, toast was being burned for the household, same as usual.

How had she got in without me hearing? Had they kissed, said sorry, and made it up? Was their love for each other strong as mountains once more?

When she brought up my bowl of porridge, I asked, 'Why did you have to argue last night?'

'Argue?' she said. 'What a funny idea. You must have dreamed it. Father and I *never* argue. Arguing's very bad manners, worse than licking your knife.'

How could it be? She'd told us that holding your cutlery in the wrong hands was the worst bad manners of all. Another time, she'd said it was putting your elbows on the table. Another time, it was answering back. How could one ever know where the true essence of polite manners lay?

All day I watched her closely from my position on the trunk for telltale signs of re-departure. If she walked out once, it could happen again. Or perhaps, next time, it would be he who stepped away into the windy darkness and never came back?

And which would be worse?

Which parent did one need most?

It had been a terrible discovery that one couldn't take anything for granted, least of all the parents' love for one another. All night, too, my ears were on guard for sounds of discord. How I wished I was still contained by the secure blue bars of childish innocence.

Eventually, unable to hold the secret of the quarrel any longer, I told Mary what I'd seen and heard. She was unimpressed.

'Don't you believe me?' I said.

'Course I do. But you know you shouldn't have been poking your nose into other people's business. It's wrong to pick up fag-ends.'

She failed to understand that I hadn't been eavesdropping, that their quarrel had been forced upon me. I said, 'I was the victim.'

She said, 'It's normal, them having quarrels. That's why

they go out to the pub so much. So they can do it in private without us watching.'

I said, 'But they're supposed to love each other. Solid as a rock, Father said.'

'Fighting's part of grown-up love,' Mary said knowingly. 'You'll understand when you're older.'

Would I? I wanted to understand now. Since Mary wasn't offering me much support I confided in our grandmother what I'd seen and heard.

'Oh, *that* man!' she said with a sigh. 'It was hopeless from the start. I'm *sure* she only married him to irritate me.'

What did my grandmother mean? Although I pressed her, she wouldn't explain more.

'Least said, soonest mended, my dear. No use crying over spilt milk. The Lord has his ways. Better make the best of a bad job. Now then, Ruth my dear, as soon as they let you up, I'm hoping you'll be able to come and stay with me for your convalescence. Would you like that?'

'Oh yes please, Granny.'

A few months after the windy night row, Veritas had a new baby which, as Mary explained, proved conclusively that they loved each other at least some of the time. The student lodgers greeted its arrival by showering the hall, stairs and front steps with fresh rose petals which lay pink and pretty for the first few days, then turned brown and crackly.

Our father beamed happily into the potato basket, still tied with blue ribbons as there was no money to waste on

39

pink, and he made strange whistling noises through his moustache to entertain his third daughter. Having an extra mouth to feed didn't make our parents any better off but did make them happy. They had no time to argue either, let alone go out to The Drayman's Arms.

The wife of a rich neighbour sent round a hamper of food. 'It's instead of flowers,' she said. 'In view of the circumstances.'

'Anybody would think we're starving European refugees,' I said. I didn't like being patronised.

'But look,' said Mary. 'It's from Fortnum and Mason!'

'What's that mean?'

'The poshest shop in London.'

'So the proverb's true!' said Veritas excitedly. 'Every new baby *is* born with a loaf of bread in its mouth. You unpack it, girls. Choose something delicious for your supper.'

But when Mary and I opened the hamper we found nothing as sensible as a loaf of bread to put in a baby's mouth.

Quails eggs in aspic, Italian olives stuffed with almonds, Quince jelly, Truffles in pâté, Ortolans in brandy. I read the labels on the tins. This food was so exotic I'd never even heard of it.

Mary had. 'Yeergh,' she said. 'Disgusting grown-ups' stuff. Probably aphrodisiac too.'

'Aphro–what's?'

'Stuff lovers eat to make them obsessed with each other. Aphrodite's a goddess of love.' For someone who didn't read, she knew a lot more about the world than I did.

Since there was nothing in the hamper to our taste, Mary and I ate toast and dripping for our tea, same as usual. Our parents enjoyed the amorous gift-food. Mary was correct about its effects. Eleven months after the last baby, Veritas had another. This, Mary pointed out to me, was proof that certain aphrodisiacs really do work.

'Just as well we didn't eat any,' I said. 'I don't want any babies.'

'I do,' said Mary.

FIVE

Death Hath No Dominion

On a bright morning as the sparrows cheeped on our front railings, and the spring sunshine illuminated the streaky grime of our back windows, Veritas announced her latest theory on child-rearing.

'Children of the New Elizabethan age should not be reared in the city. It's bad for their health and their development.'

Growing children required the pure air of the countryside to inflate their lungs, the freedom of the fields to exercise their limbs.

Veritas was ready to put theory into practice. We were moving. While our father looked admiringly on, she organised our mass evacuation from London. The student lodgers and the old fur coat were left behind. Five children, a lot of books, two typewriters, and an old storage trunk were transported by train to a romantic farmhouse which, like everything in their lives, was way beyond their means. The sprawling building stretched from the west wing to the east wing, encompassing numerous oak-beamed rooms, large and small, from the tiny priest's hole cupboard hidden behind the main chimney breast, to the vast stone-flagged dining hall. In between were parlours, sculleries, kitchens, a play-scale theatre in the attic, outhouses and barns. All was surrounded by paddocks, woodlands and lush water meadows where horses grazed.

'They're not horses,' said Mary gazing at them with a mixture of adoration and envy. 'They're called ponies. There's a subtle difference.'

Within hours of our arrival, she'd become a dedicated animal-nurturer, acquiring a pet duck and a mongrel puppy, both of which now followed her wherever she went like a pair of trusting toddlers. But their devotion was not sufficient and Mary yearned for the affection of a pony too.

'They look like horses to me,' I said.

'Only because you're ignorant.'

Whatever branch of the equine family they were from, I didn't care for creatures which nipped you when your back was turned, and ran away if you tried to climb up on to them. Mary didn't have the same objection. She scrambled easily on to their broad backs and trotted them around the meadow.

Their owner was our nearest neighbour. Miss Creake was brown and leathery, with a wispy piebald fringe and large yellow teeth very like her ponies'.

'And we have our very own deathwatch beetle,' our

father said approvingly of our new home after he'd heard the insect's quiet ticking inside the mighty beam above the main door.

'Why's that good?' I wondered.

'Because the larva of the deathwatch beetle never makes its home in timber which is anything but rock-solid. It guarantees this house will stand firm for at least another five centuries.'

This was reassuring.

But just because a house stands firm for five hundred years doesn't mean that the people inside it will. I wasn't to know that the Grim Reaper, armed with his trusty rusting scythe, was already striding purposefully along the lane towards our happy family and that within twelve months, one of us was to die.

However, even if I had known, I wouldn't have had to worry because when love is stronger than mountains, it endures even beyond the grave. (Or so Veritas had told my little sisters as we buried their tortoise.)

'By the way, my dearest sweetheart, have you thought of a plan yet?' our father gently asked our mother after we'd seen to the tortoise funeral.

'A plan, dearest?'

'Yes, my love. The plan about how we will afford to live here.'

'Why yes, my darling. I've loads of ideas,' she replied blithely. 'We won't go hungry. There's lovely fresh vegetables in the garden. Mary's been digging up some potatoes. And if I don't sell anything this month, I certainly will next month. Till then, we'll fall back on our assets, won't we?'

By assets, she meant the twenty-four fruit forks in her trunk. So the forks were unpacked and admired for their intricate if pointless beauty before being sold at the weekly auction in the nearby market town.

Our silver christening mugs were also unpacked, not to be auctioned but to be used as everyday milk mugs. For a few short months we became, or at least lived the lives of, comfortable country folk. Veritas's fancy black hat was not needed in this new life where we had our own cherry trees which would soon produce real cherries.

At last I had a bedroom of my own with lattice windows from which I could watch swifts swooping through the balmy air feeding on airborne bugs, and I could brood, from a safe distance, over ponies grazing in the sunset.

Meanwhile, though Mary hadn't yet got hold of a pony of her own, she'd added two white Silkie hens, a pair of guinea fowl, and a lame goat to her circle of furry and feathered admirers.

Veritas and our father were also enjoying this rural dream. As though they had not a care in the world, they sat in deck chairs under the flowering fruit trees while their toddlers romped in the daisies beside them. Perhaps they were trying to make the most of what little time was left. Perhaps they were all too aware that the deathwatch beetle was known as a portent of death, that to identify its sound was to hear your own death warrant.

The life of bliss was brief. Within months of arriving in the new home, our father died. So much for the healthy benefits of fresh air and open fields.

Veritas was strangely buoyant. She didn't seem surprised. And she insisted that he hadn't gone very far.

'But what on earth's going to *happen* to us?' I wailed.

'Nothing,' she said with inspiring though unconvincing confidence. 'There'll be no change. We'll carry on just as though Father was here. In fact,' she went on, warming to her theme, 'in many ways he *is* still here! He's going to go on being with us and looking after us for ever!'

'Of course he won't!' I snapped. I was angry. I knew from reading novels that when a father dies, there should be much wailing and weeping and gnashing of teeth. But Veritas didn't encourage torrents of emotion. She wanted us to hide grief away where it wouldn't show.

'Wailing like housemaids is undignified and spoils your complexions,' she said.

Bad news travelled quickly through the hamlet. It reached the ears of our neighbour, the pony-breeder. Miss Creake came trotting through the rain, tethered her mount to a tree, stomped up to our front door, rapped impatiently on it with her riding crop. I answered it.

'Your pa's dead,' she said. Was this a question or a statement?

'What?' I said.

'Your pa's dead, yes or no?' Ah, a question.

'Yes. Early this morning,' I said and burst into tears.

'He borrowed a book,' said Miss Creake, ignoring my sobbing. Or so I thought. In fact, she was entranced by it.

'A first edition. Very rare. On dressage in the cavalry. Soon as you've sorted things out, I'd like it back.'

I started to close the door. She held it open with her riding crop.

'Of course, m'dear, shame for your ma and all that. But . . .' She paused, then began speaking out of the side of her mouth as though somebody might be listening in the bushes behind. She looked even more like one of her ponies. 'Shouldn't say this, but between you and me, m'dear, it's for the best.'

'Oh,' I gasped. But how could somebody's father being dead possibly be for the best?

'Don't tell the old girl I said so. Well, good afternoon to you.' She strode back to her pony. 'And the book,' she called back. 'Don't forget.'

'No,' I replied stiffly. 'Thank you for lending it. I expect he was very grateful.'

With the prickling still behind my eyes, I told Mary what Miss Creake had said.

'And it *isn't* for the best, is it?' I said, wondering if something more awesome had happened which I didn't yet know about. Perhaps our father had gone mad just before he died, or blind, or had to have both his legs amputated? Then, possibly, it just might be said to be for the best. I knew that people said 'It's for the best' about newborn malformed babies if they died. But not, surely, about people's fathers?

Mary clutched Friendly, her favourite hen, more tightly in her arms and she shook her head. 'Of course it isn't for the best. How could it be?'

'Then why did she say it?'

'Maybe she thought that Father and our mum spent too much time with each other and not enough with us. Old Creakie's never had a husband. She doesn't know anything about anything, except ponies.'

Thank goodness I had a wise sister to comfort me.

Once the funeral was over (Miss Creake did not attend, though she raised her riding cap respectfully after the hearse containing the coffin when it passed her in the lane), Veritas returned with renewed vigour to writing the pageants and fictions which might pay the rent.

'It's so easy with your dear father's hand guiding mine all the time,' she said. 'He sits beside me at the desk. Can't you feel him, Ruth?'

Did she mean his ghost was actually in the room?

'Don't worry,' Mary told me soothingly. 'It's just the shock making her off-balance. It'll wear off.'

But it didn't and our father's memory was kept boisterously alive. His portrait, showing him wearing a bow tie, an overgrown moustache and a straw boater tilted rakishly to one side, was hung above the kitchen range so that none of us – especially the younger ones – would forget what he looked like. His suits still hung in a cupboard (though now with mothballs in the pockets). His bed, next to our mother's, remained made up as though he might at any moment return. His ink-blotter and his paper stapler stood on his desk just where he'd left them the last time he used them.

Now that she couldn't talk to him all the time, Veritas talked about him instead. We learned more about his past than when he'd been alive.

After World War Two, he'd been doing important work to save the population from the gloom of Austerity. Before that, during the war, he'd done dangerous, secret work to help combat Hitler. Before that, he'd been a famous playwright and a celebrated poet. Before that, a sought-after film adviser, and before that, a glamorous film star in silent movies. Before that, a tough jackaroo on a horse on a sheep station in the Australian Outback. And before that, it was the First World War, when he'd been a courageous soldier fighting on the North West Frontier.

You name it, he'd seen it, done it, been there.

'Probably,' said Mary slowly, for she was as wary of our mother's handling of historical truth as I was.

Our father wasn't around to confirm or deny the events of his life. We had to accept Veritas's version or nothing. It was most unsatisfactory. I resolved that before I grew up and had children, I would set down a clear and accurate record of my life so that there could be no doubt about what I'd done, and who I'd been. I'd have liked to start working on it immediately. The trouble was, I hadn't yet done anything and I didn't yet know who I was.

I went up to my room to get started on my homework. We had to write an essay called 'A Day in the Life of a Threepenny Bit'. I'd had to write a similar one in my last school. I knew that the life of a small yellow coin was long but tedious. I decided I'd do better to get started on my own life story instead.

SIX

The Do-Gooders

Our father must have been born, like Venus, out of a cockleshell, leaving no trace of parents or other relatives. Veritas, however, was part of an enormous extended family. She had hoards of long-lost friends too. Friends and relations now began to turn up to offer advice, to bleat over her sorry plight. We became pitiful exhibits in a Freak Fair.

Veritas welcomed any visitors. She called it 'dear pals rallying round'.

'Vultures descending, more like,' Mary said. 'They're only coming to gawp.'

Neither of us liked the descent of interfering adults telling our mother what to do when we were here. Were we too immature to be of use in deciding the family's future?

Posh friends sent boxes of cast-off clothes, not outworn, not outgrown, merely out of fashion. Sweeping coats, satin evening gowns, clothes so grand none of us could wear them – apart from Alfred George, who unpicked the fox-fur collar from an elegantly flowing opera cloak to wear over his grey shorts as a loincloth. Aunt Thrift sent us her daughters' outgrown underwear.

'How terribly kind she is,' said Veritas as Blanche pulled satin brassières, elasticated waspies, boned basques, powerfully strong corselettes out of the parcel and tried to work out how to put them on.

'They're no use to any of us,' I protested. 'Because whoever they were bought for is a very unusual shape.'

'Not ìbought forî, Ruth! "Made-to-measure" for. Look at the label. They're from the Queen Mother's very own corsetière.' Veritas was impressed. We weren't.

Three people (Veritas's brothers) sent useful money. The rest offered what they believed was reliable wisdom.

'Darling!' screeched her hysterical friend Denise. 'You simply must remember to eat properly! That's the only thing that matters!'

Denise, who was thin as a poplar tree, with a voice like a strangled cat, brought with her a bunch of black grapes delicately cradled in tissue, a bottle of gin, and a small ceramic jar marked *Patum Peperium* which contained a tiny quantity of something brown and salty.

'Looks like squashed cat poo,' whispered Alfred George.

'Short-lived luxuries,' muttered Mary disapprovingly.

'We have to keep her spirits up,' said Denise. 'With such terrible times she's going through, the poor darling.'

'What about us?' I said. 'Aren't we going through them too?'

'Sweetie, you've got youth on your side,' said Denise, tweeking my cheek, then ordering my brother to bring forth fresh thin toast for the *patum* and two clean glasses for the gin.

'Ice too, dear boy!' Denise called after him.

Alfred George came back with two china mugs but no ice. The only available ice in our household was the frost on the window-panes.

'Poor darling magnificent Veritas,' Denise crooned. 'I don't know how you're managing your wonderful creativity with all this lot to look after.'

Veritas explained about our father's hand helping hers along the page. I wished she wouldn't. But Mary told me that if it made her feel better it was all right.

Denise didn't find it odd. 'And does he *speak*?' she asked eagerly. 'Because he must! You must make him. I know the most adorable clairvoyant who could do wonders for you. You'd have to pop up to London, but well worth the expense. If you could only hear your dear husband's voice, your writing would take off into the stratosphere.'

'Her pageants don't earn us very much,' I said. I was beginning to suspect that we'd be better off if Veritas wrote less rather than more. 'And they need simply reams and reams of paper. It'd be best if she concentrated on shorter things which didn't use up so much paper.'

53

I had in mind those jingles for advertisements she used to write, and verses for greetings cards. They made money. I said, 'Or how about short pithy articles about country life?'

'Your mother is a creative artist, not a hack,' Denise said sharply, and she began the arrangements for Veritas to meet the fortune-teller who would be able to see what can't be seen and hear what can't be heard. I wished I was older. I wished people paid attention to me.

Our father had been dead for six weeks when the first of the suitors turned up. He was a retired colonel from the village. He paid a formal call to advise the Widow Veritas that, in her penniless state, she should immediately place her orphans for adoption, put the past behind her and, unburdened by dependents, start her life afresh while she still had a reasonable innings.

'And you'll not be short of offers, dear lady, of that I can assure you,' said Colonel Buckstaff, tapping his nose with the stem of his pipe.

He invited her out for a drink the following week.

'She's not really going to go, is she?' I asked Mary.

But she was. She washed the typewriter ribbon ink off her fingers, combed her hair, dabbed brilliantine along her eyebrows to make them full and glossy. Then she borrowed my bike, pumped up the back tyre which had a slow puncture, and pedalled off towards the The Ploughshare.

'I expect she's lonely, poor thing,' said Mary with a sigh.

'She's got us,' I said defiantly. I didn't like the way so many adults considered us to be a sad burden to be coped with or, worse, disposed of. Veritas needed us. Through us, she could hold the memory of the true love of her life.

Veritas may have intended to go alone to The Ploughshare, but minutes after she'd left, Alfred George, wearing the fox loincloth and with our father's bone paper knife tucked into his snake-buckle belt for protection against lions, went trotting down the lane after her.

'Good idea,' said Mary approvingly. 'He'll be like a guard dog.'

Thus it came to pass that Colonel Buckstaff didn't get further than buying Veritas half a pint of best bitter and starting to tell the tale of how he'd nearly lost a leg in a minefield in Tripoli before the chaperone turned up. Alfred George began tapping on the frosted glass windowpane of the Saloon Bar and calling out that he was thirsty.

Veritas returned home early, pushing my bike. Alfred George was balanced on the front handlebars with the red stain of Cherryade all round his mouth.

'So how come *he* always gets bought fizzypop when we don't?' I grumbled to Mary.

'Because he's a lonely little boy who hasn't had a treat for ages,' said Mary gently.

Perhaps she was right. She and I at least had each other for security, just as Blanche and Felicity had one another, whereas our brother had only the imaginary lions in the woods to rely on.

Veritas's bossy sisters, Aunts Thrift, Charité and Speranza, came again to tell Veritas how to cope with widowhood. None of them were widows. They had opinions nonetheless.

'Now do listen properly, Vee. The first priority,' said Aunt Speranza firmly, 'when bringing up a large family, is enough good servants.'

'Enough good parents might be more useful,' I muttered.

Mary glared at me angrily. 'Don't say that sort of thing! You didn't really want her to get entangled with some buffer like Colonel Buckstaff, did you?'

'Course not,' I mumbled.

'That's right. It'd be grim. Just imagine having to be nice to some stranger because he was your stepfather! Anyway, that Denise woman says if anybody's going to be married, it'll have to be one of us.'

I thought that sounded just as grim. 'I hate all the lovey-dovey muck,' I said.

Colonel Buckstaff's personal plans for our mother were efficiently eclipsed by Aunt Speranza's domestic plans. A tidal wave of distressed gentlefolk were about to flood our lives. They were Aunt Speranza's solution to what she saw as The Servant Shortage.

'Her name's Janice,' said Aunt Speranza. 'From a well-connected church family. She wanted to work with the poor in some foreign slum. I told her parents that helping you would be useful practice.'

The would-be missionary didn't get up till midday. She had to wait till the boiler had been stoked so that there'd be hot water for her morning bath. Most of us had a bath once a week. Doing it every single day seemed a waste of time, energy, water and soap. After her bath, Janice liked to set her hair in bobby pins, lacquer her nails and shave her legs. I'd never heard of women shaving.

When Janice finally came downstairs, she was smoothly decorative rather than useful and quickly caught the eye of Colonel Buckstaff on one of his courtship visits. Thanks to Aunt Speranza, Janice was replaced.

Our home was no longer a rural paradise. It became refuge to a succession of general helpers who were convalescent, or on probation, or had been jilted by their fiancés. Two arrived together by taxi, unannounced.

'We're actresses,' said the blonde one.

'Then I don't expect you'll find much work round here,' I said.

'But we heard your mother was a playwright,' said the platinum one.

'Pageants,' I said. 'For youth groups. Always with an uplifting theme.'

'Uplifting?' said the blonde one.

'Doing-as-you-would-be-done-by, loving your neighbour as yourself. That kind of thing.'

'Ah,' said the platinum one. 'We'll give it a try.'

At least they kept Colonel Buckstaff out of our mother's hair.

No one could be paid a wage so few did much helping. All required a great deal more caring for than Alfred George, Blanche and Felicity put together.

With all these well-intentioned women turning up in order to not lend a hand, Mary and I had to work hard. They needed beds making up for them, early morning cups of tea, late breakfasts, deck chairs on the lawn. Mary and I hardly had time to go to school.

Mary didn't mind. I did.

'I'm missing so much. I'll fall behind.'

Veritas said, 'Surely a bright girl like you can mug it up overnight?'

'Mum, I cannot swot up the whole sweep of history in one evening. Nobody could.'

'Why ever not? Look at Princess Elizabeth. She didn't go to school at all, and *still* ended up as Queen of the Realm!'

Our father had been an enthusiastic royalist. Out of respect for his memory, now Veritas was too. Or perhaps, thanks to the expensive clairvoyant, our father had been whispering Tables of Succession into our mother's ear.

I said, 'Unless I find a spare king to marry I'm highly unlikely to turn into a queen. I'll have to earn my own living. So this afternoon I'm going to mend the puncture on my bike, and from tomorrow I'm going to school every single day, at least till the end of the week.'

'Very well, Ruth, as you wish,' said Veritas sadly. She seemed to prefer to have us with her at home, not only for company but to keep the household running.

Since none of the volunteer helpers would touch any of the heavy outdoor jobs, Mary and I had to do them. Mary liked machines. She took over the grass-cutting, front and back, upper and lower. Her method of mowing was noted, by one of the actresses from her place in the hammock under the trees, for its natural artistry.

'Machines are stronger than humans so it's just a case of letting the machine lead the way,' Mary explained before she went careering diagonally across the lawns, swinging round the boles of trees, leaping over paths and rockeries to create sweeping green patterns like the raked gravel of a Japanese garden.

I didn't like handling the mower. I couldn't understand how it worked and its noise and thrusting power frightened me.

I didn't much like seeing to the stoves either. The big boiler either roared like a hungry dragon or went cold and sulky like the Minotaur skulking in his labyrinth. I specially didn't like filling up the hods with fuel.

As I made my way stealthily across the back yard towards the tomby blackness of the coal shed, the wind moaned through the yew tree. The tawny owl squawked. Rats rustled in the rafters. I heard the phantom clip-clopping of hooves on the ground. I sensed heavy breathing right behind me, and even felt it blowing hot on my neck. Fast and frantically, I shovelled fuel. Working quietly made no difference. The spectres would find me anyway.

SEVEN

Things That Go Eek

Out of the corner of my eye, I caught sight of a luminous shape fluttering at the shed door. A pale disembodied hand reached round the doorpost. My lungs squeezed tight. My heart thumped. As I emerged from the shed with two hodfuls of anthracite, the hand grasped me by the throat.

I knew that hand. It was from *The Riddle of the Handless Corpse*. Cousin Cormorant had smuggled me in to see it. It was X-certificate so I'd worn a wide-brimmed hat and heavy lipstick.

'You'll love it, Ruthie,' Cormorant promised. 'It's really gruesome. Loadsa gore.'

The bloodstains had been in black and white so hadn't seemed scary. But in the coal shed there was no Cousin Cormorant to protect me. I ran for the safety of the kitchen door with the translucent hand right behind me. I staggered in. Veritas asked with some surprise, 'What on earth's happened?'

'I saw something,' I stammered.

'What?'

'I dunno. Some kind of ghost.'

'Oh Ruth, you big baby. You know there's no ghosts.'

Blanche, sitting up at the table eating her toast fingers for tea, said, 'Thereth no ghoth ecthept for the Holy Ghoth. An the Holy Ghoth alwayth thtays inthide church and ith kind and good thpethially if you thay your prayerth.'

If a child of four wasn't scared, then I shouldn't be. 'Oh well,' I said, trying to make light of it. 'If it wasn't a ghost, it was probably just some common or garden ghoul.'

Blanche, like our mother, was always eager to see the bright side of life. 'Yeth! Ith a Boggart!' she crowed excitedly. 'Ruthie's theen a boggart. Thath oneth a good thpirith, whooth helpth people to their jobth.'

While I raked out the grey ash from the bottom of the boiler and filled up the top with fuel, I entertained Blanche by telling her of other supernatural creatures which might be lurking outside. There were Bogeymen, Goblins, Hobgoblins, Banshees, Voodooists, the Midnight Stalker, the Grim Reaper, the Mad Axeman, Shuck the Headless Dog, and perhaps also the Hunchback of Nôtre Dame. Blanche giggled so much that she pushed a toast finger up her nose instead of into her mouth.

'Really, Ruth,' said Veritas. 'I think you *like* making people frightened. You're probably hoping there really is a big man outside waiting to jump at you.'

I slammed down the cast iron lid of the boiler.

I said, 'Are you so brave you haven't *ever* been afraid of the dark?'

'When you've lived through the Blitz, you know you'll never be afraid of anything again.'

Not even a lifetime of widowhood? I wondered. But no, she didn't even seem afraid of the long future. I couldn't help but admire her optimism, misplaced though it was.

Mary was more phlegmatic. 'It's only because she hasn't any choice. It's sink or swim.'

Yes, Veritas was definitely swimming, breast-stroking defiantly through the waves of adversity.

A new admirer began eyeing up the inmates of our household. From my bedroom window I noticed, each morning, a faded velvet riding hat bobbing along below the hedge-top. I heard the snorting and heavy breathing of her mount. Miss Creake was on the prowl. She took to exercising her favourite chubby skewbald down the lane alongside the west wing of our house. Sometimes she stood up in the stirrups and I saw the long horsy face peering eagerly over the hawthorn twigs.

What was she looking for? It can't have been her book. I'd long since taken it back. Perhaps she was casting an envious eye at our orchard as fresh grazing for her quadrupeds.

One morning as she was gazing longingly up at our house, she caught sight of me, Rapunzel, at my window. I was plaiting my hair. This had to be done as regularly as a man shaved his chin. In the Upper Fourth, brave new styles were being invented to test the uniform regulations. This week, instead of two symmetrical braids dangling like cat's tails on either side of our heads, we wore four, five, seven or eight plaits, all tied with standard navy blue ribbons. It drove the Latin teacher, uniform controller, wild with frustration for there was no written rule against it.

Miss Creake bared her teeth in a yellow grin. She waved her riding crop towards my window in a heathen salute.

In Veritas's codes of conduct, it was Bad Manners to ignore a grown-up's greeting. Even if they pestered you, adults were always right. Reluctantly, I gave Miss Creake a half-wave with my hairbrush. Then I ducked out of sight.

Next morning when I heard trotting hooves in the lane, I dived for the floor. Not fast enough. She'd seen me. She hallooed enthusiastically. However much Veritas might reproach me for my lack of good manners towards my elders and betters, I didn't respond to the repeated shouts.

That afternoon as I returned from school, free-wheeling, no-hands, in through the gates of home, Miss Creake stepped out in front of me. I had to jam on the brakes to avoid running her down.

'Oh,' I said. 'Are you all right? I'm terribly sorry.'

If only I had said nothing.

'M'dear, got a load of horse manure for you.'

'Manure?' I said.

'Present for your garden. I'll bring it down in the horsebox. You tell me where to tip it. Well rotted. Ready for use. Make all your pretty flowers grow.'

'I don't do the garden.'

'Ah well. Good day to you.' She walked off on her bandy legs like John Wayne.

She thought up another pretext for calling. She brought me a sackful of rotten apples. 'Drops, m'dear. Windfalls. Thought you might like them to make a tasty apple pie.'

They were so rotten that even her ponies had refused to eat them. I took them and dumped them on our compost heap.

'She's only trying to be kind,' said Veritas, 'because she knows we're on hard times.'

Soon, it was an offer of riding lessons. I explained that we didn't have money for that kind of thing.

'Free, m'dear. Nothing to pay.'

I should have told her that I disliked the feel, the smell, the hairy touch, the bad breath, the vicious temperament, the hefty hoofy feet, and the blunt, lawn mower strength of ponies.

'Thank you, Miss Creake, but I've got a lot of homework,' I said. 'I expect one of my little sisters might like a ride.'

'I'm not offering lessons to *them*, dammit. I'm offering them to *you*.'

Miss Creake wouldn't give up. Her fixation on me was, if not as strong as a mountain, as strong as a tussocky hillock. She lay in wait all afternoon. As I pushed my bike up the last hill before the joyful free-wheel spin home, she jumped out from behind a tree. She caught hold of my handlebars. She pushed her riding crop between the spokes so I was immobilised. She placed her horny hand on my shoulder. She smiled so that her big teeth showed like a row of yellow bricks. Her breath smelled as strong as a pony's. Did she eat grass out of solidarity with her animals? I wished I was like a crab, hidden inside a hard carapace to protect its soft parts from attack.

Miss Creake made her offer.

'What d'you say to a job, m'dear? Saturdays. Couple of hours. Need a strong gal about the place. Help me in the yard, clean the tack, y'know the drill.'

Trembling, I whispered, 'No thank you.'

'I don't expect somethin' for nothin'. I'll be payin' you, gal. I know you need the cash.'

The moment she removed her riding crop, I scuttled for home. I confided the whole horror to Mary. 'And I think she's in *love* with me,' I said. 'It's creepy. You should've seen the way she leered. And she kept wanting to touch me.'

Mary said, 'Her ponies are very sweet when you get to know them, specially that old lame piebald. I've been sketching him in the paddock.'

'*You* go and be her stablehand then!'

'It's not me she wants.'

When Veritas heard about Miss Creake's offer, she said, 'How really kind. I hope you said yes. It'd be nice for you to earn some pocket money. Gosh, I'd have given anything for a Saturday job at your age. But Mother wouldn't allow it.'

I explained that I didn't mind working, and to prove it

I'd got myself a Saturday job washing up beer mugs in The Ploughshare, and that it was Miss Creake I objected to.

Veritas said, 'It's just your hormones, Ruth, making you imaginative and edgy.'

It wasn't.

Veritas said, 'Be sensible, Ruthie. You've got to learn to be more open-minded now you're growing up. The world's full of all types and they're all God's children.'

If growing up meant being leered at by horsewomen then I didn't want to do it. I wished I didn't have these soft squishy breasts developing in front of me which made me look like a woman even though I didn't feel like one.

Blanche said, 'I think Mith Creake thinkth you look juth like a little pony yourthelf. Coth you got thutch pwetty hair.'

Mary glanced up from her sketchbook. 'Blanche's right! It's all the little plaits! That's what's turning her on. It reminds her of a pony's mane groomed for the gymkhana.'

I said, 'You mean I look too tomboyish?'

Mary said, 'If you want to put her off, you could try and make yourself more female. Look at what you're wearing!' (One of my father's khaki-colour ex-Army shirts, and a pair of Alfred George's grey socks.) 'And doing your hair like a corn dolly is hardly feminine, is it?'

'I don't want to be a fully feminine lady. I just want to be me.'

Occasionally, Veritas tried to be a real mother. When I went up to bed, I found a printed leaflet tucked under the eiderdown where I'd find it. It was called, *A Chat with the Doc: So your Daughter is Nearly a Woman!* It was the usual old stuff about spots, periods, armpits, and changing moods.

Mary's advice was more practical.

'These might help,' she said. She tossed into my room the women's magazines she'd found, discarded but well read, in the blanket-fluff under Miss Blonde and Miss Platinum's beds. Now I could learn how to brighten up my afternoon dresses with a double string of plastic poppit beads, how to create filmstar kiss curls and fat tulip lips like Zsa-Zsa Gabor, to pluck myself svelte theatrical eyebrows just like Ava Gardner's in her latest red hot rôle. And I could follow, step-by-step, the Young Miss Busy Beauty Calendar to become a little lovelier each day.

Oh yes! How I longed to be lovely enough to be admired by the right sort of someone.

'Ruthie darling, you're lovely already! Everybody adores you!' Veritas tickled my neck rather as I absent-mindedly tickled the ears of Mary's dogs.

Veritas didn't understand. I meant *really* loved, not just by a mother, some sisters and occasionally, if he wasn't out in the woods building hideaways, a brother.

Unexpectedly, it was not the new, svelte, feminine me, but Alfred George who released me from the unwanted attentions of Miss Creake. He stalked her round the lanes, just as she kept stalking me. He lay in wait for her behind a haystack.

'Then I jumped out at her,' Alfred George told me

proudly. 'And I told her if she ever annoys you again, I'll stab her through the heart with my dagger and show no mercy.'

'Your dagger?' I said. I didn't know he had a dagger. And I certainly didn't think he ought to have one.

'It's only an old butter knife. Quite blunt. But she didn't know.'

'Thanks,' I said. So he did have some use after all.

A new ghost arrived to haunt me. I was woken early one morning by an overwhelming sense of loss, of fear for our family's future. Alone, in bed, was the only safe time for grief. Veritas didn't like it if we cried for our father.

'It sets a bad example to the younger ones. Just remember all us poor girls in wartime. *We* didn't see the people we loved for years at a time. And *we* didn't cry. *We* put a brave face on it.'

Through my tears, I noticed a figure sitting at the end of my bed. Young, male and asleep. I was too surprised to go on feeling overwhelmed with sadness.

I lay still so as not to disturb him for, as Veritas had often told us, 'A man's rest is sacred. The cruellest thing a woman ever can do is to wake him while he sleeps. When a chap's been up on the roof all night protecting us from incendiary bombs he deserves a bit of sleep.'

The young man on the end of my bed wasn't protecting me from anything. I was nonetheless glad he was there. When I woke in the morning, he'd gone.

Three nights later, he was back, breathing though still

lying doggo. He became an erratic visitor, sometimes there, sometimes not. He made no demands, never spoke, though occasionally he'd wake, look at me, direct, sincere, and seem to smile. In the half-light it wasn't clear.

Those other ghosts flitting around the coal shed had all been, I now realised, Miss Creake on the prowl. But what was this one? Was it an ancestor of the farmer who used to live here?

Mary slept with two dogs on her bed. I told her about the shadowy man on mine.

'That's a dream lover,' Mary said as though she knew all about it.

'I wasn't dreaming.'

'You don't have to be asleep to dream about men. It's quite normal while you're young.'

'What should I do about him?'

'Don't worry about him. Once he knows a real person has fallen in love with you, he'll just go away.'

From the matter-of-fact way she dismissed it, I sensed she'd long since outgrown dream creatures and was impatient for the real ones.

But where were they?

RIDING WITH THE TIDES

EIGHT

Summer Stagger Swing

When you go to school with five hundred girls dressed in drab serge gym tunics to be instructed in life by thirty-two women in beige twin-sets, you don't get much chance to mingle with men. It's the bunchy clothing that puts them off.

'That's their aim,' said Mary. 'To make us as ugly as possible, lest we fall into sin.'

The one male in our midst, Alfred George, was unlikely ever to have useful male friends dropping in to see him because he dressed so oddly and anyway preferred being on his own.

He'd taken to wearing a thick rope coiled round his waist and, tucked into it, the blunt yet potent butter knife with which he had vanquished my foe. Every afternoon, he disappeared into the woods. He stayed lost till late into the night. Mary said it was normal for a boy who was missing his father. Veritas didn't even seem to notice.

Solemn Felicity was also growing up strange. She'd taken to collecting stones.

'Oh, my dear little long-lost daddy rabbit!' she said each time she picked up a new one. She kept these treasures inside her mittens which were on a string threaded through her coat-sleeves so that she wouldn't lose them and get chilblains. The mittens clanked stonily along the ground behind her. Veritas didn't notice. Mary thought it was normal behaviour for a youngest child who was missing her father. The noise meant we would never lose her.

Meanwhile, bubbly Blanche was growing cuter every day, with her mass of red hair sprouting out like a glorious halo of fire around her head. Even Colonel Buckstaff, to whom most females under fifteen were invisible, noticed Blanche.

'Lovely little lass,' he said. 'Tell your ma she ought to think of putting her on stage. Make a spot of cash out of her.'

But Blanche could never become an actress, however cheerfully undamaged by fatherlessness she was. She wouldn't be able to say her lines, or not so anyone could understand. Her lisp was getting worse by the day, and almost by the word.

I told the man who sat at the end of my bed, 'If only I lived with a family who were normal.' He nodded and seemed to understand.

Mary must have thought so too. As soon as she was fifteen and could legally leave school, she did.

'I'm not going to be a secretary to some boring man.

I'm going to study art,' she said firmly. The art college was twice as far away as the school, but she pumped up her tyres and never complained it was too far to pedal.

At art college, it seemed the more bizarre a person's home life, the better they were admired, adored and maybe even loved. Boys in big floppy jerseys and paint-spattered dungarees, their fingers stained dark with Indian ink, followed Mary home in twos and threes and even fours, to sit around in our kitchen drinking black tea. Blanche, Felicity and I were hugely impressed. Veritas kept an open mind, for these admirers were not the loud-voiced, baying young men in cavalry twill slacks and trilby hats, whose papas were estate managers and solicitors, that she had had in mind for us.

Early one morning I was knotting my navy-blue tie in a cunning new triple-knot which would, I anticipated, make the uniform-inspection teacher wild with fury since there was no written definition of an authorised knot. As I glanced from the window to check that Miss Creake wasn't out there ready to deliver me another unsuitable gift, I was surprised to catch a glimpse of Mary in the garden. She was half hidden in the dawn mist. She seemed to be dancing.

Later, when I went to fetch my bike from the barn, I saw her again, barefoot, drifting through shafts of apricot sunlight around a clump of blue delphiniums.

It wasn't the usual sort of thing she did, particularly when there was so much pollen about.

'What on *earth* are you doing in the flowerbed?' I called.

She smiled a strange, distant smile. Then I saw she wasn't alone. Sitting cross-legged amongst the flowers of the herbaceous border was a young man with wild curly hair, a trumpet, and a real black beard. None of the boys who'd followed her home so far had been old enough to grow proper beards.

'Where'd you find him?'

'Up the caves,' she said.

Where was that?

'He's a jazz musician.'

I could hear that. And I had no idea that a trumpet could play so softly. Mary danced as though bewitched.

I pedalled away across the dewy garden and off to school, sneezing all the way, highly perturbed.

What did it mean? Dancing in the delphiniums with a daft look on your face wasn't something that had featured in the *So your Daughter is Nearly a Woman!* leaflet from the chemist.

Yet again, Mary had taken a huge leap forward into maturity and left me behind. She'd outgrown her affection for fowls of the air and beasts of the earth and transferred it to human males. Some days she was so busy drinking tea and talking about art with her fellow students that she even forgot to feed the hens. Felicity and I had to do it for her. She seemed to have outgrown her hayfever too.

Veritas noticed but wasn't alarmed by the new kind of people in Mary's life. Natural optimism took over.

'We must ride with the tide,' she proclaimed at breakfast, and was so impressed by her own liberal outlook, that by tea-time she'd begun writing a new pageant on the theme.

'Based on the changing ways of young people in the late fifties,' she said.

I peered over her shoulder at the page on the typewriter.

'*Long gone are the days of arranged marriages for our lovely daughters,*' she'd made one of her characters say.

'What on earth d'you mean?' I said. 'Long gone are arranged marriages by about five hundred years. There haven't been any in Sussex since the Tudors. You make it sound as though they only stopped having them last week.'

Blanche said, 'Ith meant to be like poetwy. Thee meanth young ladieth thethe dayth don't want to be thtuck in a romantic rut no more.'

'That's right,' said Veritas. 'I'm trying to show how we should all drift with the tides of social progress.'

'Before, you wrote "ride with the tide",' I said. 'Which is it meant to be?'

'Drift with the tide, ride with the tide, swim with the stream,' said Veritas waving her arms about in the air to demonstrate her approval. 'They're all good. The main thing is to see how times are changing. The whole world is changing, forwards and onwards. And we must change with it. And if modern mothers don't want their daughters to stay out all night they should encourage them to bring their friends home, however alien they appear.'

'That's not what you said when Peter and Geof and Spud

and Finger turned up to see Mary last Sunday.'

On Friday nights, Mary and her art-loving mates went Up the Caves. Soon, I was old enough to go along too.

'So long as you can pay your own entrance fee,' said Mary. 'It'll cost you half a crown.'

In Veritas's mood of change, I had her wholehearted approval. 'It'll do you good to meet some nice young things,' she said. 'It's exactly what Father would've wanted. He was well ahead of his time. He mixed with highly Bohemian types too. He used to say he didn't mind who his daughters married, even an out-of-work drummer, so long as he was a thoroughly nice chap.'

I tried to explain that going Up the Caves wasn't about meeting chaps with a view to marriage.

'What ith it for in the caveth then?' Blanche wanted to know.

'We go for the music,' I said loftily.

It was almost true. Mary went so she could gaze at the man with the trumpet.

'And what do you do? Do you danth?'

'Not much, no.'

'Do you thing then?'

'No.'

'Talk?'

'It's not like a cocktail party,' I snapped.

Blanche turned to Felicity and said, 'I exthpecth Ruthie doethn't want to thay what they do becauth they kith a lot. That'th what boyth and girlth do.'

NINE

Travelling Tune

Mary's enthusiasm for loitering in a damp cave full of hot music was on the wane. Her artistic horizons began to expand. She was having visions of other places to be.

One afternoon, after I'd been hanging about in the Public Reading Room pretending to do my homework, I went to meet her outside her art college. She led me over to the Black and White Moo-Cow Milk Bar, sat me on a high stool, and ordered two frothy coffees.

'I've a plan,' she said.

'Good,' I said, slurping up the froth off the top of my cup.

'We don't need boys. Or men. Or love. We need to go travelling.'

'Ooh! Where?' I thought she meant somewhere daring like Brighton. I said, 'Bronco Roll and his Merry Jazzmen are playing at the Pavilion.'

But her vision went a lot further than that. From her duffel bag she took a map, unfolded it reverently and spread it across the counter. In the top left-hand corner was a small bit of Sussex printed in yellow, with the blue of the English Channel next to it. Then came the whole of Europe, veined with scarlet roads. In the bottom right-hand corner was some blue sea dotted with tiny islands.

'That's where. And to as many places as possible in between. Paris, Florence, Rome – it's all there. I have to touch the cradle of civilisation.'

'The what?'

'Athens. Where Western art began. I don't want to go alone. There's all the difficult languages on the way. So I was hoping you'd come.'

'I can only do a bit of French and some Latin.'

At the grammar school only very intelligent girls were permitted to study German. As for learning Italian, that was considered far too racy.

'That'll do to start with. So will you come?'

'But what about that nice man with the trumpet? Wouldn't you rather go with him?'

'Him? Far too pushy.'

'Or that other one you said looked like a magpie?'

'No way. I told you, I'm off all of them.'

'So when then?'

'Soon as possible.'

'I'm supposed to go to school.'

She said, 'You're not at school now, are you? And you don't like it when you are there. You're always bunking off. Travelling the world offers a much broader education.'

I knew she was right. 'But I've only got twenty-five quid in my Post Office book.'

'That'll be enough. Travelling saves money.'

I didn't see how.

'Because you don't have time to go shopping for frivolities. And because in France the government subsidises bread. Italy's incredibly cheap too. You get thousands of lire for every pound.'

We had to get Veritas's permission to be allowed to apply for passports and, until we reached twenty-one, we'd have to ask her every time we wanted to leave the country.

Luckily, she was in one of her equable moods, especially when Mary pointed out how it showed enterprise to attempt a trip and tenacity if we ever arrived anywhere, and that we'd both develop a greater understanding of everyday economics than she'd managed to teach us.

'Just so long as you promise to stick together all the time,' Veritas said. 'And don't fall in love with anybody I wouldn't approve of.'

'That's not what Mary's looking for,' I said haughtily. 'It's all about finding art.'

Mary and I packed our duffel bags.

'Basic necessities only,' Mary said. For her, this included her sketchpad and inks. I took dictionaries in Italian, German and Greek and a volume of John Keats's poetry. His sonnets seemed to be about Greeks. I reckoned reading them would put me in the right mood.

Our grandmother was so thrilled that she presented each

of us with a five-pound note.

'My dears, how it brings it back to me. My mama took me to Florence to see the great masters. You will visit all the galleries, won't you, darlings? And look out for the mimosa.'

'Mimosa?'

'Such a colour. Such a scent. It grows all along the Riviera. Quite splendid.'

Not everybody was pleased.

Veritas's friend Denise arrived with some cast-off clothes. She said they were Dior.

'Last season's, but I'll never wear them again.'

They were pink and slithery, quite unsuitable for a rural pageant-writer. Even as Denise was measuring up hemlines, I could see Veritas working out if they'd cut up into a few useful lampshades, some fancy cushion covers and a couple of little dancing tunics for Blanche and Felicity.

Mary tied a GB motor badge to her duffel bag before slinging it over her shoulder.

Denise was appalled when she realised what was going on.

'They want to go hitchhiking?' she shrieked. 'You're crazy, Veritas. Letting young people loose on the Continent is just asking for trouble.' She began reeling off recent disasters, derailments, bus crashes, civil disturbances, earthquakes, kidnappings in various corners of Europe.

I said, 'I know we'll be safe. Granny's going to have us prayed for every Sunday during Mattins.'

So we kissed our mother goodbye and set out. Denise was still shrieking. 'But Veritas, where will they stay if you haven't even booked them into any respectable *pensione*?'

Getting to the nearest sea-port was easy. Cousin Tern had just passed his driving test, and turned up behind the wheel of his father's Hillman Husky. He was highly pleased with himself. Mary easily persuaded him that Newhaven was only a short way off his route home. He drove us past loading cranes and warehouses, right to the ferry ticket office by the harbour wall.

'Gosh,' he said, looking both alarmed and envious at the sight of the grey choppy sea. 'Gosh, absolutely spiffing. Auntie Vee's a real brick, isn't she? My ma would never let me try this kind of caper.'

We thanked him and hurried off to buy our tickets. Foot Passenger Returns to France: two pounds each.

The crossing took four hours. I noticed another foot passenger. He was wearing a real French beret and an artist's smock. His luggage was four unwieldy canvases which kept blowing over on deck.

'That's Jack,' said Mary. 'From college. Only he likes to be called Antoine. He's a right show-off.'

Antoine seemed more surprised to see Mary than she was to see him. Antoine seemed pleased. He told us he was going to Paris to sell his paintings and that his long-lost godfather was due to pick him up at Dieppe.

'Would you like a lift? I'm sure Georges won't mind. His Peugeot's simply vast.'

We accepted. On arrival on French soil, we followed Antoine across the cobbles to Le Café du Port to wait for the godfather. Antoine ordered a round of drinks, *citron pressés* for us, brandy for himself, before realising that he hadn't managed to go to the purser on board the steamer to change his money into francs. Luckily we had. Mary paid for the drinks and for the *sandwiches au jambon* which Antoine said we needed. Our first day's budget was quickly spent.

We passed several hours which felt like a lifetime in the bar listening to Antoine telling us about painters he'd heard of, waiting for his godfather to turn up and watching a light drizzle fall.

I thought, we could be doing this at home. It was no surprise when the promised lift to Paris never materialised.

TEN

Off The Map

We spent the night in a camp site. It was within sight of the ferries going back to England. That seemed the easiest thing to do. We had our return tickets.

Mary said, 'I always knew he was a fake. Even his paintings are copies.'

I established our first rule of the road. 'Don't pal up with old acquaintances.'

Mary agreed. 'And never trust a man in a French beret who offers to buy you a drink.'

Next morning we were on our way once more, walking sturdily down a straight road regularly lined with shady trees. Everything looked delightfully foreign. Today the sky was blue. The foreign sparrows were tweeting in French. The fields had a quaint Gallic charm. The only thing missing was traffic. But we had our baguettes which had cost only a few centimes each to chew on.

A rickety van came up behind us. We put out our thumbs. The van passed. It slowed. It stopped. It waited for us to catch up. The driver was an elderly lady in a battered straw hat and blue worker's overalls. She asked where we were going.

'*Direction sud*,' I said. Towards the south.

The lady invited us to climb in. She was a fruit farmer. She was returning home from market. She had been selling the cherries from her orchard.

'You are English,' she said.

Since I already knew this basic fact, I didn't feel I had to respond, apart from nodding vaguely.

'I have been waiting fifteen years. It is my desire to invite you to share the *déjeuner*.'

Mary and I had made a second rule of the road, which was never to enter strangers' houses. I whispered, 'She seems a bit crazy but I think she's safe.'

Madame Dupont lived with her maid in a modest villa. It was surrounded by neat metal railings and cherry trees. The maid was told to set the table for two guests. From the fuss the maid made, there couldn't have been guests very often.

Le déjeuner was leek soup, rabbit casserole, dandelion leaf salad and Camembert cheese. I whispered to Mary in English (since that was the only language she was willing to understand) that as Madame Dupont was eating the same food, it couldn't be poisoned. After the cheese, Madame Dupont stood up. She wished to make a speech.

'I thank you, dear *demoiselles*,' she began. She raised her glass in the air. 'I will drink a toast. I salute you for your brave acts.'

I translated what she said. Mary muttered, 'What's she mean? We've never met her before. We haven't done anything.'

'And I salute your brave countrymen. It is for what they have done for me.'

Tears gathered in Madame Dupont's eyes as she began to describe the sound of bombing from the coast, the rumble of tanks, fighting in the fields and byways around. I could understand just the top ten per cent, but I sensed her fear and relief. The liberation of Normandy was nearly fifteen years ago, yet she made it sound as though it was only the other week.

'Mister Churchill is not here. You must be the representatives of your country. The English twice have saved my life. In the First World War when I was just a girl. And then they came again, as you have done, across the Channel so that we might live in peace.'

I tried to point out that we hadn't had much to do with winning the war, but she needed to thank somebody and we'd do. So we might as well accept with good grace.

'*Allez!*' she said. 'Go now. Enjoy our beautiful France.'

She filled our pockets with cherries, pressed us to take the remainder of the Camembert and showed us to the door.

'Four brave young boys, your compatriots, sheltered

for a few hours in there,' she said, pointing to the barn beside her house. 'I gave them soup. There was not time for more. You will find them up the hill. They are there forever.'

A mile beyond her house, in open countryside, we came to the gates of a walled cemetery. They stood open. We looked in. The grass was neatly clipped, not a blade out of place. On it were set, with military precision, line after tidy line of identical white headstones. I gazed in awe at the sheer quantity. Mary drew them. The graves stretched to the distance. Each had the name and age of a soldier. Many were no older than Antoine or our Cousin Tern. I wondered if any of those young dead soldiers had been hoping their first trip abroad might be a bit of a caper.

France looked different after that. Sharper, keener.

We soon got the hang of the hitchhiking. We were speeding south. We invented some more rules of the road. No hitching after sunset. Always follow our route on Mary's map so we'd know where we were if a driver decided to take a deviation. Always keep our luggage to hand in case we had to disembark at short notice.

This happened during a lift with a country doctor. He was on his way to visit an old countrywoman who lived in a hut at the very top of the mountain. I was, as usual, sitting in the front because of Mary refusing to speak. She sat in the back. She had the map. She was following our route.

'Not far now,' the doctor said. At least, I thought that was what he said. His teeth were clenched as though he'd caught lockjaw from a rabid dog. Instinct made me anxious. He was not a reliable man.

'My sister and I would like to descend from your vehicle, if you please, sir,' I said.

He didn't hear.

I said it again, adding, '*Immédiatement!*'

He still didn't stop. He was trying to go faster. It was a steep road. We were facing uphill. The pastures of the Massif Central were passing more and more slowly on either side.

Over my shoulder I said to Mary, 'This lift's no good. We have to get out. Don't forget the bags.' Her head was resting on them. She was dozing.

'Out!' I snapped at her. She woke. I opened my door. I flung myself towards the slow-moving verge. So did she. We and the bags rolled down into the flower-filled meadow.

The driver-doctor made a rapid U-turn, swore at us through the window, and went screeching at full speed back down the road. There was no sick old peasant further up the mountain.

Two new rules of the road were added. Both of us must stay awake and alert. We mustn't take a lift with any vehicle which stopped for us before we'd started hitching.

After two weeks, we reached the Mediterranean. The glare was so bright that Mary got sunstroke. We had to spend travel funds on sunhats. Shops in Cannes were numerous. They were called boutiques. The hats were à la mode. Mary's had gold tinsel round the brim. Mine was a saucy sailor boy's cap in pink gingham with rosebud trim. They did not have price tags on them. They cost as much as several hundred baguettes.

In a perfect camp site perched on a rocky hillside overlooking the sea, dotted with silvery olive trees, we were attacked by mosquitos. We had to buy anti-insect coils to burn like incense inside the tent.

Near Monte Carlo, we had to find a pharmacy to buy sanitary towels. This should have been straightforward, but it was difficult. I didn't know the word. It wasn't in my dictionary.

Mary said, 'Well, mime it then.'

I wouldn't. The pharmacist was male.

I should have bought some aspirin too, but I wanted to get out quickly. I had such acute stomach cramps that I felt as though I could hardly stand up straight, let alone walk.

Mary said, 'Remember what Mum says.'

Veritas used to try to comfort us by saying that the cramps of periods were Mother Nature's way of preparing women for childbirth. 'The pains of labour are no worse. They merely go on for longer.'

Heroically, Mary shouldered both duffel bags while I trudged miserably behind. She bought me a *croissant au chocolat*, breaking her rule of silence towards French people.

'It's to raise your morale,' she said. Her tender concern had the same effect as lying in bed with a hotty. I quickly recovered. I wondered if chocolate croissants would have the same effect during real labour.

When we saw starlets splashing in the shallows at San Tropez and millionaires' villas set amongst palm trees and purple-flowering bougainvillea, I was wide-eyed with wonder. When we saw vibrant canvases by Chagal, paper cut-outs by Matisse, chapel ceilings painted by Tiepolo and Titian, Mary was silenced by joy. Together, and equally, we were impressed by Etruscan tombs, medieval frescoes, classical arenas, amphitheatres, Saint Peter's Square. We saw the seven hills of Rome, and the ancient paving of the Appian Way. We saw Mount Vesuvius and the sleeping volcano. We wandered down the crowded back-streets of Naples. Mary said they looked as though they'd been drawn by Hogarth. I said they looked as though they'd been written by Charles Dickens. We boarded the aft-deck of a ferry and sailed through the Corinthian canal, so narrow we could almost touch the sheer rocky sides which glowed like gold in the sun. And when we'd reached the cradle of Western civilisation, we bobbed around the wine-dark seas in fishing smacks, from one island to the next, to find more treasures.

So much freedom, so many beautiful things.

We met, and Mary drew, donkeys, mules, stray dogs and hens, old women in black. We met, and I tried to speak to, French and Italians, Dutch and Danish, Spaniards, Canadians and Catalans, Australians and Austrians, Greeks and Cretans.

Mary's sketchbook was filled with her drawings, and

bulging with pressed flowers, scraps of coloured sailcloth, dried leaves, dead insects, fossils and opalescent snail shells she'd gathered on the way.

Occasionally, as we queued outside a youth hostel, I listened to the travel-chatter of so many languages and I thought back to the graveyard in Normandy. Our freedom had been won at such a high price.

One soft evening we sat on the cool marble steps of an open-air theatre. It was two thousand years old. It was still in use. We ate our black olives, white crumbly cheese and bread. A flock of goats and their goatherd scampered over the rocky slopes. The cypress trees hissed in a faint breeze. I thought we should stay there forever. Mary said, 'Eat up. Time to go home.'

'What?' I said. 'We've only just got here.'

She didn't mean home to the hostel. She meant home to Home.

I said, 'But we haven't been to Delphi to see the navel of the world. And if we went up to the Bosphorus we could visit the Topkapi Museum.'

I wasn't ready to go back. I'd never be ready. I'd found what I wanted to do for the rest of my life. Travel. Explore the world.

Mary shook her head. 'It's time,' she said. 'I can feel it in my bones.'

She could feel that love was stronger than mountains. All types of love. We were tied to the end of a long piece of elastic. We'd stretched it as far as it would possibly go. Now it was pulling us back. We must put the glaring sun, the shady museums, the bleached sails of the windmills, the cool marble, behind us, turn north towards the grey, soggy island of home.

ELEVEN

Got Them Moving House Blues

I'd expected Veritas to be a whole heap more pleased to have us back, safe within the bosom of the family. Her reaction was mixed and most of the mixture was on the negative side.

'It's no good!' she said. 'It's got to stop. Immediately.'

'What's got to stop?'

'We can't go on like this.' She began to fling her arms about, not to embrace us but more like a trainee traffic-director, first in one direction, then another.

'Like what?'

'Living like rich people. Going off on expensive Grand Tours of Europe as though you were eighteenth-century aristocracts.'

Did she know how unreasonable she was being? 'Listen, Mum,' I said fairly patiently. 'It cost us thirty-seven pounds each, we've been away for weeks and weeks and we've even brought back some change.' (I didn't say that this small change totalled eleven hundred Italian lire and two Belgian francs, none of which had any purchasing power in a Sussex hamlet.)

'And *another* thing!' Veritas went on with more over-excited arm-waving. 'All this gallivanting round Europe has set a terrible example to the younger ones. Now they think they can go wandering off any time they like. I never know where they are.'

What about all those theories of juvenile independence?

Things were definitely in a big mess. Mr Bradsack, the grocer, hadn't been paid for over a month. And Mr Bluefinch hadn't been paid his rent for three months. Alfred George was wearing a pair of my hand-me-down shoes that were two sizes too small for him so his toes were all scrunched up.

Where, before, Veritas had been gently riding along with the Tides of Change, now she was being buffeted out to sea by swift Currents of Improvidence.

'Riding with the Tide is a luxury we can no longer afford,' she said sternly. 'We've gone way beyond the point of small economies.'

Her small economies had, so far, included cutting up a perfectly serviceable blanket to try to make a school overcoat for Blanche, taking the bulbs out of most of the light fittings to save electricity (so we kept tripping on the stairs), and cancelling the daily milk delivery (which Mr Bluefinch anyway ignored).

'Children got to drink milk,' he said glumly. 'Else they don't grow proper. Just look at that poor lad's toes! He needs a drop or two of milk to straighten them out. Dare say she'll pay when she pays.'

I knew he was right. Trying to save the price of three pints of milk a day wasn't going to change the direction of the sinking ship.

'So we'll have to think up something more drastic,' said Veritas.

She'd always been good at thinking up things. It was one of her greatest qualities. She now proved specially good at thinking up drastic things, such as dividing the house with hardboard partitions and subletting one half to a rich visiting American who would be impressed by the beams and not notice the absence of heating. The essential drawbacks were that it wasn't hers to divide, and that we didn't know any Americans who liked oak beams.

Then she thought of selling something. But apart from her creative fictions, what had she got to sell except for five dented silver Christening mugs, which were not hers but ours? She thought of opening Tudor-style tearooms.

'I'll make fairy cakes and drop scones,' she explained. 'Mary and Ruth will be the waitresses. I'll run you up some pretty little pinnies and caps.'

The plan floundered when Mr Bradsack refused absolutely to let her have any cake ingredients on tick.

Just as well. We all knew that edible cake-baking had never been her strong point, though her versatility with multi-coloured icing sugar was renowned.

Finally, the most drastic plan of all.

'I'm going to speak to Denise,' she said. And before we knew where we were, the broom of Denise's clean sweep had bustled into every corner and was catapulting Veritas into a Big Move.

'And she's found me a flat. Very compact, an absolute gem, she says. Isn't she a dear?'

'A flat?' Nobody roundabout lived in a flat. Nor up in the main village. There weren't any. People lived in damp cottages or draughty farmhouses.

'Not here. In London. And surprisingly central so that influential people will be able to drop in any time they want. It'll be ideal for making contacts.'

'Contacts? What sort?'

'So I can get more work. Denise says she thinks she can wangle me a commission to write about modern cookery. Won't that be fun?'

I said, 'You'll never be able to afford the rent.' There was no point in reminding her she didn't know how to cook.

From the speed of events, it seemed that Denise had been plotting this evacuation even while Mary and I had been admiring marble edifices beside the Aegean Sea.

Veritas said, 'Of course she had to do it quickly. She's off to New York any day now. She's going to leave us all her soft furnishings. She's such a dear.'

I said to Mary, 'We should never have given Denise a chance to infiltrate like this. We shouldn't have gone travelling and left Mum on her own.'

Mary said, 'I *had* to go. It's been an investment for my

artistic future. I've got a real job all lined up. As soon as I've got my diploma.'

She was to be the set designer's assistant's assistant in a theatre in the Midlands. 'It's called the Theatre Royal. Tom works there.'

'Who?'

'Tom. I've told you about him loads of times.'

I was sure she hadn't.

'He's the set carpenter. He looks like a macaw.'

I didn't ask which aspect of a macaw, but I could guess.

'My first show's going to be a Restoration comedy.'

I made dark mutterings about rats leaving sinking ships when they should be sticking together.

'Don't expect me to follow any of you,' I said, and went off to live with my grandmother.

She was poor as a church widow. I had to get a job immediately.

I found one as apple-sorter in a market garden. My boss was surprised how much I already knew about apples, that I could tell a Souring from a Seedling, a Reinette from a Hanwell. He'd have offered me a permanent job but the work was strictly seasonal. So I went to work as a hotel chambermaid until The Mitre went broke. I took the driving test in my grandmother's Austin 7 and became a van-driver for a toffee factory. This led to my becoming clerical assistant to an importer of Indian felt slippers, where I learned to type rather better than I learned to do accounts. So I bought a second-hand typewriter and in the evenings, while my grandmother dozed before the fire, I wrote short stories about toffee factories and slipper-importers. I sent them to magazines. Sometimes they got accepted and I felt a few brief moments of satisfaction, but it never lasted. Not until I'd started writing another story.

My father had not recommended story-writing as an occupation. Though the memory of him was sometimes distant, his axioms remained clear and loud.

'I would not wish the life of the writer on any one of my daughters, and certainly not on my son. It offers nothing but poverty and pain.' He'd said it cheerfully enough but that same morning his play about Mary Queen of Scots had been returned, unread, though stained with coffee-rings, by the impresario to whom he'd sent it.

Within six months I'd started, finished, been sacked from, or walked out on seventeen jobs. No moss grew on me. I knew it never would. I was just a no-hoper rolling stone.

One morning, as I glumly surveyed the three-minute soft-boiled egg which my grandmother had thoughtfully set before me, she said, 'I believe, Ruth darling, your mother's been missing you. Isn't it time you went up to town to see her?'

Yes. It was.

So I took my typewriter, half a dozen speckled eggs and a jar of my grandmother's bottled plums, and I set off on the train, with my bike in the guard's van, to seek my fortune in the Big Smoke.

Goodbye Granny. Goodbye green and muddy Sussex.
Hello Mum. Hello sooty city.

TWELVE

Into The Rhythm

The bijou flat was in a mews above a lock-up garage. It was more of a gentleman's pied-à-terre. There was a cocktail cabinet which lit up and played the Nutcracker Suite when you opened it, but no fridge. There were sumptuous dusty velvet swags and pleated pelmets round the windows, but no curtains. The bathroom was tiled in stylish black marble but there was nowhere to do a family wash, let alone hang it up to dry. The boudoir had pink moiréd walls, soft pink lighting. The other bedroom was more of a walk-in wardrobe.

Veritas and Felicity shared the pink room. It was also Veritas's study. Alfred George and Blanche had bunk beds squeezed into the wardrobe-sized room which they shared with two hamsters and an ugly caged bird with a broken wing.

The flat was already crammed to overflowing. There definitely wasn't room for me and my bike too.

'Of course there is,' said Veritas, shoving my father's army camp bed into the crevice between her work table and the pink bed. 'It'll be fun, all hugger-mugger, just like during the Blitz when we had to sleep in the underground stations, all lined up along the platforms.'

Felicity didn't have a bed. She was on the old storage trunk.

'I'm a horse,' she explained.

I wondered, was pretending to be a horse progress or regression from collecting stones?

'And this is my loosebox, which is just the type of bed a horse likes.'

I remembered my own indignity about having to sleep on top of that trunk. Felicity had a tougher time than I ever did. She was complaining less.

We were so tightly packed that night that if one person sneezed, we all felt the tremor. In the morning I set out job-hunting. I knew what I wanted. It definitely wasn't apple-sorting. Nor importing felt slippers. Despite my father's warnings, I pedalled confidently eastwards, towards Fleet Street. That was where the newspapers and journals came from. I padlocked my bike to a lamppost near the Law Courts, took a big breath, tried to look tall, mature and confident and strolled up to the first office I came to.

A doorman stood guard outside. His uniform was double-breasted, braided and gold-buttoned. I asked if I could please go in to speak to the editor.

'Not without an appointment you can't, duckie,' he said.

I tried at the next newspaper building. I got as far as the

vestibule. That editor was busy too. After I'd walked to the entrances of and even got into the vestibules of a further twelve offices, I was unexpectedly granted permission to pop up to the deputy features editor.

'Come in, come in! Don't hang about wasting time,' she barked. She was smoking a mauve cigarette in a holder, and had four telephones on her desk. Two began to ring simultaneously.

'I suppose you can type?' she shouted into the phone, though the question was meant for me.

'Yes.'

'What's your w.p.m.?'

I had no idea. 'The usual,' I said.

'Shorthand?'

'Yes,' I lied. Surely fast scribbling was nearly as good.

'Telephone proficiency?'

'Of course,' I said. Using two at once, as she was now doing, was doubtless an easily acquired knack.

'Yerh, yerh, yerh,' she was saying into one mouthpiece. 'It's going to be OK. I'm interviewing our short list right now.' She turned back to me.

'And do you have a flair with words?'

'Yes. Very,' I said. I knew that even if I sometimes didn't, Veritas always did. I could borrow some of her flair.

'Are you interested in people?'

'Hugely interested,' I said with what I hoped was an interested, alert, perceptive, sensitive, yet detached expression.

'Yerh,' she said.

My technique must have worked. She offered me a job.

'Start tomorrow. You'll take over "Dear Eve". Yerh. Right?'

Dear Eve?

'Wonderful,' I said. 'Thank you very much.'

Outside, I bought a bunch of golden yellow chrysantheums for Veritas, three nets of gold-foiled chocolate coins for the children and a copy of the publication of which I was now an employee. I pedalled speedily back to the mews flat.

'Fleet Street?' said Veritas. Why did she have to sound so incredulous?

'Not quite. Just off. More like Fetter Lane.'

'Not a major newspaper then?'

'No, Mum. It's the young-hearted magazine for bright everyday women.' I was quoting from the front cover. 'There's knitting patterns and crochet, and kitchencraft, and short stories and quick quips.'

'Whath a quick quip?' Blanche wanted to know.

'Like a handy hint, only shorter. But that's not my page. I'm going to do "Dear Eve".'

I showed them the page. Dear Eve's photograph was at the top. Dear Eve looked auntyish, fortyish, reliable behind horn-rimmed glasses.

'She answers readers' letters about their problems,' I explained.

Dear Eve was now me. Or I was her. The photograph was very old.

'They must be desperate,' Alfred George muttered as he unpeeled a chocolate coin and fed it to the injured crow.

'I think they are,' I said, though I didn't find out till I started work that I'd only got the job because the previous Dear Eve had eloped with the knitting pattern editor.

When the crow had had its fill, Alfred George began munching his way through the rest of the chocolate coins.

'Thanks for the choc anyhow,' he said. 'Maud really appreciates it.'

Maud blinked a malevolent eye at me and shuffled to the back of her cage. I should have known it was an omen of dark things to come.

I bought myself a pair of false eyelashes and an alarm clock. I started my new job.

Veritas's enthusiasm for having so many of her dear ones clustered round her bed began to wear off. It was harder for her to reach the rickety table under the window that was her desk.

'Time is money,' she said. 'Every second counts when you're trying to earn a living.'

It was time for me to leave the nest again.

I trailed round the streets, peering in the newsagents' windows. Alfred George came with me. I was looking at the FOR RENT cards. He was looking at ads for odd-job boys. He found a newspaper round. I found a single room two streets away. It was £4 a week. I could just about afford it. Alfred George came with me to check it out. The room was tall and looked out on to a brick wall.

'Bit dark, isn't it? You'll go blind,' Alfred George said.

'I won't be here most of the time. I'll be in my nice airy office.'

The room had moulded plaster cornices on the high ceiling, a kitchen sink in one corner, a gas cooker on legs in the other and a terrifying landlady.

She stood, arms akimbo, in the tiled passage as Alfred George helped me move in.

'And what, may I ask, young lady, d'you think you'll be doing with them books? They'll only be harbouring the dust. I like to keep a hygienic lodgings here.'

She was suspicious of the typewriter too. 'I'll have you know, I won't stand for no undue larking about on these premises. And none of them loud records to be played after ten neither.'

Alfred George reassured her. 'It's all right. She never types at night and she doesn't have a gramophone.'

'Very well. Rent, Fridays. Four weeks' notice. Toilet down the passage, second left. Bath, second floor. Water hot Tuesdays and Thursdays, five-thirty to six-thirty. Leave as you would hope to find. Consideration for others is a virtue.'

'Yes. Of course.'

Alfred George decided not to antagonise her further by wheeling my bike in. He chained it to the railings of the church opposite.

'You can always move it further down the road if it looks

as though there's going to be a wedding.'

The hardest part of my new job was opening seven hundred letters a week. The rest wasn't difficult once I'd got the hang of setting up my copy for the printer. It involved a whole new sign language more complicated than any shorthand. The woman who wrote the 'Dear Doc' page showed me how.

'Money for jam, your page, isn't it?' she said.

I could see she was no more Dr Gavin Ashe than I was Dear Eve. But thinking like a doctor was, to her mind, part of the job. Her scope was wide.

'I came in as an audio-typist,' she explained, 'and when I took over Dear Doc, it was nothing but neuralgia and haemorrhoids. But now I'm pushing back frontiers.'

She'd covered readers' schizophrenia, artificial insemination and brain tumours, malignant and benign. 'I'm planning on marrow transplants before the end of the year.' If readers didn't write in with ghastly enough illnesses, she wrote the letters to herself as well as the replies.

On Friday afternoon, I got paid. On Friday evening, I went to have supper with my family. I took a fresh pineapple. We had candles on the table. Felicity and Blanche brushed their hair. Alfred George washed his hands. It was a celebration.

Veritas had cooked the recipes in that month's cookery column. It was entitled Cooking At Sea.

'And my main dish is Deep Sea Irish Stew à la Mode. I invented it myself.'

Felicity asked, 'What's "à la mode"?'

'It means "sort of"', Veritas said. 'So it's only sort of Irish stew.'

Blanche asked, 'What'th in it?'

'Taste it and guess,' said Veritas.

'Chicken?' said Felicity.

'Anchovies?' I suggested.

'TVP!' said Veritas triumphantly. 'It's a new invention. Russian spacemen in satellites are eating it even at this moment. It's what the whole world will soon be eating.'

By candlelight the flat, cramped and draughty though it was, looked quite cosy and the Textured Vegetable Protein recipe was surprisingly successful. Veritas had been right to move. It was all working out well. She was joyfully riding with the tide once more.

After supper, I helped the children with the washing-up, then with their homework, and I went back to my independent room feeling comfortable and confident. Compared to the complicated muddles Dear Eve's readers suffered, my own family were rock-solid settled. I could get on with an exciting London life of my own. I'd start going to poetry readings, visiting art galleries, maybe join an evening class.

I got a picture postcard of Trafalgar Square to send to Mary. '*Got new job. Family all A1. Everything hot diggety dog. love, Ruth.*'

I should never have written that. It was tempting fate. Something was about to happen to Veritas which had never happened before. She was about to fall dangerously, mortally ill.

Even if I'd understood the meaning behind the disabled crow's prophetic gaze, I could have done nothing to hold back the huge tidal wave which was pulsating towards us.

THIRTEEN

When Darkness Covered The Earth

Early mornings in my room were dark and dank. So were evenings. Alfred George had been right. Weak daylight barely penetrated, sunlight never. One normally dark morning, just as the alarm clock clanged me awake, Felicity came bursting in like a little ray of sunshine. She neighed and tossed her mane. Her satchel – correction, saddle-bag – was slung over one shoulder. She seemed less solemn than usual. Being a horse was obviously good for her.

'Ruthie! I'm glad you're here,' she said, snorting dramatically. 'I cantered all the way down the street. I've been knocking and knocking at the front door for ages. She's really horrible, that fat lady.'

She flung herself down to recover from her encounter with the landlady.

I said, 'Oughtn't you to be on your way to school? You'll be in trouble if you're late. That'll get Mum in trouble.' I tried to sound stern. 'It's essential to profit from education while you have the chance.'

I got ready for work. This meant loads of eye make-up and a wig. My own reddish frizz didn't have the right gravitas for Dear Eve. A sharply geometric brunette bob gave me more maturity though it was a daily struggle to get it on straight.

'I *am* on my way,' Felicity said. 'But Mum told me to come. She wants you.' She pulled out the dental brace that was meant to be round her front teeth, wiped it on her blazer sleeve and put it away in her pocket.

'What, right now?' I had to be the other side of St Paul's by ten, where dozens of anguished problems awaited me.

'I know. But she said to try and catch you.'

'What for?'

'I think maybe it's private ladies' stuff.'

I said, 'You mean she's got a period kind of tummy-ache?'

'Dunno.'

Felicity was still far too young to know from personal experience how bad stomach cramps could be. However, not trusting Veritas to be any more informative to her younger daughters than she had been to her elder ones, I had explained the reproductive process to Blanche and Felicity myself. (Though not to Alfred George. He'd found out from the hamsters.)

In a breezy way I said, 'She'll be OK. I'll give her a call from my office as soon as I arrive.'

I liked a chance to use the phone on Dear Eve's desk. It never rang. Readers-in-distress were too shy about their problems to speak them into a telephone receiver. If they'd known how inexperienced Dear Eve was, they wouldn't have written to me either.

Felicity said, 'That'll be too late. She's in her bed.'

No wonder she can't keep to her deadlines if she tries to work in bed. The carbon papers get creased, and blanket fluff would get on to the keys and make them smudgy.

Felicity said, 'I left our door on the latch for you.'

'You *know* you shouldn't do that! Anybody might get in.'

'Somebody did. One of those American soldiers. Blanche found him. He was sitting on the kitchen stool. He thought he was in the dancing club next door. He was ever so polite. He just waited.'

'I hope you told him to go away.'

'We let him finish his tea first.'

'His *tea*? What d'you mean?'

'He asked for a drink. He said "please". So Blanche made him a cup of tea. He tried to pay for it, but Blanche said she'd only used half a teaspoonful of tealeaves so it didn't cost more than about a penny. He gave us some pink bubble gum. Then he realised we weren't the Starry Nites Club. By the way, you got anything to eat?'

'You know you should eat a proper breakfast in the morning.' I'd have to give her a talk about sensible diet. But not now.

'There wasn't any,' she said.

I gave her a black banana while I finished getting my wig on, then I sent her on her way. Reluctantly, I went to see what Veritas wanted. It was going to make me very late.

She was huddled over a one-bar electric fire. She looked a bit tired. Her hair needed brushing. At least she'd got up.

'I think I've got a bit of a temperature,' she said wearily.

'Are you hot?'

'No. Cold. Would you ring the doctor for me?'

She tottered back to bed like an old woman. I thought, She should have been an actress.

I dashed down to the off-licence at the end of the road where the American soldiers bought whisky and chocolates for the girls they picked up. I bought some aspirins. I tried to buy a bottle of lemon barley water but the shopkeeper had never heard of it. He offered me Canada Dry ginger ale which I'd never heard of.

'To freshen up your bourbon,' a GI explained.

So I bought some anyway. Perhaps it would freshen up the aspirins.

I made Veritas a hot-water bottle and force-fed her two aspirins even though she said she was too sick to swallow. I thought, This is a husband's job, cossetting her just because she's feeling miserable.

It was clear she needed distracting from her swamp of self-pity. I tucked the blankets round her. I said cheerfully, 'My colleague on the next desk did a story about a man who had a temperature of a hundred and ten degrees Fahrenheit. He'd come back from Central Africa with blackwater fever. They had to put him in a bath of ice to cool him down.'

She didn't seem interested.

'I expect you've got a touch of flu,' I said generously. Actually, I thought she had a perfectly common cold and because she was never ill, she took it to be something worse.

'I'll come again this evening,' I said. I was going to kiss her goodbye, then decided against it in case her common cold was at its infectious stage.

For some reason, something compelled me to fritter my lunch hour, not in the canteen gossiping about Adam Faith's latest 45 revolutions per minute single song record, but pedalling across central London. I expected to find her in chirpier mood.

I noticed an ambulance parked at the end of the mews. I bumped over the cobbles a bit faster. I reached the flat in time to see two men carry out a stretcher. Veritas, wrapped in red blankets, lay on it. Her eyes were shut.

Her enthusiasm for entering wholeheartedly into any new predicament was admirable. And she'd always been fond of ambulances because of having driven one during the war. She liked fire engines too. But this time she'd taken her excitement too far.

Before I had time to dismount, her attendants were sliding her in through the rear doors and slamming them shut.

'Mum!' She didn't hear. I waved at the darkened windows but she was lying down. Of course she couldn't see. There was nothing for it but to follow. Going to hospital on your own was no fun even when you weren't really ill.

Luckily, the bell wasn't clanging. The driver obviously didn't consider her to be any more urgent a case than I did. When he stopped at a red light, I caught up. I overtook. I tapped on his door.

'Excuse me,' I said, 'but I believe you have my parent in there. May I come too, please?'

They let me climb in the back. One of them lifted in my bike.

'Good idea, Mum, to dial 999 if you were worried,' I said. Privately, I thought it wasteful of rate-payers' money.

'Doctor's idea,' she murmured without opening her eyes.

The attendant wasn't fooled by my stylishly mature brunette wig. He patted my arm as though I was about eleven. 'It's a grand place your mam's going, pet,' he said. 'They'll soon put her right. Don't you worry.'

I wasn't worried. I knew better than him about Veritas's ambulance fetish.

We travelled for miles. The Santa Teresa Hospital for Sick Women was over the other side of the Thames. Veritas was carried in. She lay on a trolley in a queue. She lay on a bed in a queue. She was taken away, she was brought back. I felt sure that if only she'd stop rolling her eyes and sighing she'd appreciate the attention she was getting.

I was used to her exaggerations. It was part of her nature to distort the truth. So how was I to know that this time it was true when she said she felt like death? How was I to know that when she moaned how her back ached a bit, she meant that the pain was unbearable? How was I to guess

117

that when she was 'a bit worried about the future', she meant she was so desperate that she couldn't even think straight?

She was finally put into a bed and allowed to stay there.

'She's being admitted,' said a nurse.

'Yes, but what for?' I asked.

'Further tests, dear.'

'How long?'

'Ooh that's not for me to say, is it? It'll depend on results, won't it?'

Veritas was whispering from the bed, 'The children. No one to let them in. After school. Get Felicity to gym club. Do homework. Alfred George must clean out bird cage. Poor bird. Proofs of prologue. Must correct and return.'

'OK, Mum.'

The nurse returned. 'Now you're not to keep worrying her,' she warned me. 'She's a sick little mummy and needs her rest.' She swished the curtains briskly round the bed. I was excluded.

Alfred George, Blanche and Felicity seemed unmoved to hear about Veritas. They got on with their usual after-school activities, none of which included homework or cleaning out cages.

Their main occupation was pressing their ears, all three at once, to a tiny transistor radio.

If I spoke, I was instantly told to be quiet.

'Please hush, Ruth,' said Alfred George.

'Why? Is there a saint in the room?'

'We've got Radio Luxembourg. But it's a very weak signal. We don't want to lose it or we won't know what's number one.'

'Oh. Right,' I said, pretending to understand what they were on about.

By the time I'd given them some food, it was too late to get back to Fetter Lane and make it look as though I'd been there all day. Never mind. I'd catch up next day.

For four days, Veritas was allowed no visitors. Just as well. Looking after Dear Eve and three siblings left little time for fretting about the sick. On the fifth day, I was allowed in. The invalid had found much to occupy her mind.

'Rent,' she gasped. 'Cleaning out hamster cages. Christmas.'

'Weeks away,' I said.

'But cards,' she whispered. 'And presents and stockings.'

'You don't usually start thinking about any of this till the day before. You say it takes away from the spirit. I don't know why you've got to start early this year.'

She lay back exhausted by the festive season before it had started.

'Better take my purse,' she said as I was leaving. 'You'll need money.'

'Thanks,' I said. 'And don't worry, we're all fine. The others have hardly even noticed you're not there.'

Not true. Of course they'd noticed. Felicity's chin was permanently thrust forward in a stubborn grimace. She refused to answer unless spoken to in horse talk, which was a language I didn't know. Blanche spent more time than seemed natural curled up on her bunk with a hamster under her jersey. Alfred George reluctantly dragged himself out to his paper round but then claimed he was too exhausted to clean out Maud's cage.

I said, 'That poor crow's too big to keep caged up in a flat.'

'Me too,' Alfred George muttered. 'When she's ready to fly, so will I.'

Veritas's purse was practically empty. It saw us through one more day. I asked Felicity and Blanche if they'd lend me some of their pocket money.

'We don't have pocket money,' they said.

I used to complain when I only got sixpence a week. Pity I hadn't realised then how lucky I was. I searched for the Widowed Mother's Pension Book. I discovered no orders could be cashed without Veritas's written authorisation and the claimant had to be aged over twenty-one. There was a stern warning printed inside the cover:

Anyone who knowingly makes a false declaration, or who attempts to obtain money fraudulently, may be committing a criminal offence.

Alfred George watched me dithering with a pen and was surprised by my reluctance to forge Veritas's signature.

'Look, easy-peasy, no big deal. I'll do it for you if you like.'

I was shocked, yet relieved, by how convincingly he wrote our mother's signature. Next day I cashed two more dockets.

She had an operation and was discharged. I went back to work as Dear Eve and caught up with hundreds of letters. Veritas spent three days at home, collapsed, and was sent back to hospital. This time we went less dramatically in a taxi. She was frighteningly calm.

When it was time for me to get back to see the children in from school, I said, 'Would you like me to tell someone so they can come and be with you?'

'I can't think of anyone better than you,' she said.

'But someone properly grown up might be more of a comfort. I could ring Granny and go and fetch her for you?'

'Oh no, Ruth! Don't tell Mother. It would upset her so terribly. She's too old for all this. Promise me you won't.'

So I had to promise.

FOURTEEN

Christmas By Catalogue

The days dribbled by. How much longer?

They let me visit any time I wanted now.

My lunch break was best. It coincided with her lunch trolley. I pulled the curtains round her bed and gobbled up her mince 'n' veg, her jam roly-poly. She was too ill to want any of it.

Each day she demanded fewer clean hankies and postage stamps. She gave up even her attempts to plan a merry Christmas. I stopped making jokes about people who'd died of blackwater fever.

I knew what was wrong with her.

They didn't deliberately lie. They were only trying to protect me. You could use any other word you liked – parasite, toxicity, sepsis, botulism, plague, pest, scourge, blight, canker, rubigo, dry-rot, so long as it wasn't the C-word.

I asked one of the nurses, 'It's cancer, isn't it?'

The nurse flinched as though I'd said a swear word. 'Ssh, dear,' she whispered.

'But it is, isn't it?'

'The surgeon found something a bit nasty,' the nurse said, 'so he took it out. And he hopes it hasn't spread.'

I knew about apples in the store room. One small bruise could spread its spores to destroy the whole harvest within months.

I hated going back to the flat, facing the breakfast mess, stretching out three rashers of bacon and a bag of muddy potatoes into a nourishing meal.

Who could I turn to? If only she'd taken a fancy to Colonel Buckstaff as he'd taken a fancy to her, she wouldn't now be my responsibility. But then, even if she had married him, I'd still be here wondering what to do with my siblings. The colonel wouldn't have taken them on.

I needed my own agony aunt.

Dear Eve, I would have written.
Please advise me. My loyalty to work and to family are pulling me in opposite directions. I have a new job.
I have a sick mother and younger siblings. What shall I do?

Even as I imagined myself receiving my letter, I was preparing my reply to myself. Divided loyalty wasn't the problem. Family love was. And where blood was thicker than water, then love was stronger than mountains and rocks and lava, stronger than jobs, stronger than everything. Love won hands down.

So I handed in my notice. The deputy editor said

she was disappointed in me.

'I was expecting great things. Dear Eve was a chance in a million for a young person to learn. You won't get another like it. A rolling stone gathers no moss.'

'Yes. I already know that. I'm sorry.'

Two phones on her desk began ringing. She picked them both up and waved me out of the office.

As I scraped up a last mouthful of carrots and gravy from Veritas's lunch plate, she roused herself.

'Ruth, what will you do about the little ones if I don't come back?'

'Come back?'

'From here?'

I shrugged. 'I dunno. I'll wait till Mary arrives. It depends on when her panto starts.'

The nurses started being really kind. One of them brought Veritas's pudding over to save me fetching it.

'It's a lovely treacle sponge today, Ruth. And I've given you an extra serving of custard.'

I could think of loads of things I'd rather have had than double custard.

Veritas started to ramble on about life insurance, the conclusion of which was that she hadn't any and it was too late to get any. What firm would insure her at this stage?

'You know I've had to name my next-of-kin?'

'Yes. I thought you put Mary.'

'They said it had to be someone over twenty-one. I've named Denise.'

'But she's the other side of the Atlantic.'

'She'll be back.'

'Shouldn't it be one of your sisters?'

She shook her head. 'I couldn't bear Speranza standing over me and looking smug. Or Thrift for that matter. And certainly not Charité. You haven't told them, have you?'

'No.' Though I would have if they'd been in touch.

'So when it's time to sort out legal guardianship of the younger ones, you must ask Denise to help you.'

When I left the hospital, everything outside had turned grey as though the colours of the world had been leached away. Usually, I hurried from Kennington to Paddington to be home before the children. Today the bike was like a ship in a head-wind, unable to make any speed at all. The wheels seemed jammed. My spirit was jammed too. I got off and pushed my bike across the park. The grass was grey. And the paths, and the bare trees, and the water of the lake.

I could pray as hard as I liked, but we weren't protected by divine grace. If one parent went and died, there was no good reason why the other shouldn't too.

Sorrow gave way to fury. How dare any parents do this sort of thing to their children.

I kicked at a grey litter bin. Lowering grey clouds pressed down from a snow-laden sky. A cold wind rippled the surface of the lake into little grey waves. There were no cheery kite-flyers out today, no ice-cream sellers, no old gents sailing their boats on the choppy water. Only grey seagulls screaming and wheeling over the water.

Why did she have to move to this horrible lonely city? Why did she have to let herself be ill? If only we were back in Sussex where we had neighbours – the Bluefinches down the lane, the Hares up the lane. I could call on them for a hug and a pat on the back.

I'd even welcome the horsey face of Miss Creake. I could see her trotting towards me through the park. I'd throw myself on her mercy. I'd muck out her ponies forever. I'd let her put her scrawny arms around me and squeeze me to her tweedy jacket.

Anything.

'By the way, Ruth,' Alfred George said, 'that man called for you again.'

'For me?' I felt my stomach turn over. 'Which man?'

Felicity said, 'That one with nice eyes.'

'What's his name?'

'I dunno. Didn't ask,' said Alfred George. That was the trouble with growing up in an all-female household. To him, one man was much the same as any other.

Blanche, more helpfully, said, 'He wath wearing a nithe jacket. And he hath thome bookth in hith pocketh.'

Felicity said, 'I think he's the one you went to the cinema with.'

I could think of one tedious person in cavalry twills and a deerstalker hat I'd been to the cinema with and I could think of another person that I'd said I was going to the cinema with but in fact we'd walked and talked and walked some more. Which one was it?

I asked Alfred George, 'Did you let him know where I was?'

'Course not. I didn't think he'd want to go trailing off to some institution full of groaning women.'

'Perhaps not,' I agreed. Seeing Veritas as she was now might have put him off me forever.

'He said he was going to Vienna.'

'What for?'

'How should I know?'

'When?'

'Didn't ask. Today. Tomorrow. Does it matter?'

'Did he leave an address?'

Alfred George wasn't sure. He didn't think so.

Surely, whether someone wrote down their address or not was not a matter of doubt. I said, 'How long for?'

Alfred George didn't know that either. He said, 'Mary's coming back for three days. That's good news, isn't it?'

Blanche tried to be encouraging. 'He mutht like you a lot. He waited. He that jutht there on the chair and waited and waited. But you thtill didn't come home.'

'You should have offered him a cup of tea.'

'You thaid we're not to give any more cupth of tea to thrangerth.'

If only she'd disobeyed my advice he'd still be here, sipping tea. If only I'd bothered to pedal faster. If only I'd not wasted time kicking litter bins. If only Veritas wasn't ill. And if only, if only.

Everybody had seen him except me. When I finally got time to go back to the rented room just before the tenancy expired to collect the last of my belongings, the landlady accosted me in the hallway.

'So there you are, young madam,' she said. 'Another of them men of yours been round after you.'

So he'd been looking for me here too.

'When?' I said.

'All times. Knocking at my door asking after you. Phoning me. Never stopped.'

'What did you tell him?'

'What d'you think I tell him? I told him I hadn't seen you for weeks, you'd handed in your notice, and if there were any more of his ringing me up I'd take the bleeding phone off the 'ook.'

'Thank you, Mrs McCreedy,' I said, my heart pumping with joy. So he did mind about me enough to keep trying to find me.

On my next hospital visit, the ward sister said, 'The Almoner wants to see you.'

And the Almoner said, 'I'm glad you're coping so well, dear.'

Coping? Sure I was coping, wonderfully, knowing that a young man with midnight eyes the colour of the darkest of anemones had tried to visit me.

'Because you wouldn't want your little sisters to have to

'No, of course not!' I said. 'Now stop asking silly questions.'

Felicity said wearily, 'You must do something interesting, otherwise what's the point in going?'

'All right then, I'll tell you what we do. We sort of stand around, and sort of dance, only not with anybody, and we listen and sort of look at each other, only it's quite dark because there's only candles stuck in the walls.'

Both little sisters thought it sounded wonderful. 'Can we come too?'

'Definitely not. Children aren't allowed in.'

Blanche and Felicity watched in admiration as Mary and I got ready for going Up the Caves. We back-combed our hair. We coated our lips with glistening white so our mouths seemed to be obliterated. We ringed our eyes with black. We pulled at our jerseys till they hung saggy and shapeless below our knees. Then we pedalled off into the setting sun, drawn by irresistible forces towards the sandstone cliffs above the old port.

We propped our bikes against a fishermen's hut on the beach, removed our shoes, and hurried barefoot up the steep steps cut into the cliff side. The music wafted out like intoxicating smoke. We hurried along the sandy tunnels towards it.

'Come on. Quick. They're playing the *Summer Stagger Swing*!'

It might equally have been a *Bronco Buster Roll* or a *Red Satin Stomp* for all I knew. But I felt alive.

The central cave was crowded, lit only by flickering candles. While the band played their hearts out dark figures in mock-croc jackets, narrow leather ties, and dainty pointed shoes, lurked and milled and shuffled. Eddies of mist swirled in off the sea. The tang of salt mingled with the smell of hot healthy youth. Mary and I joined the gyrating huddle of fishermen, sailors, art students, but no young men in cavalry twills seeking partners for the slow waltz.

In smaller caves there were other kinds of activity. Drinking, conceiving, thieving, flick-knife fighting, and the sharing of illegal cigarettes.

I wanted to go and have a look. 'No. We don't need to join in with any of that,' Mary told me firmly. She was right. Life was quite vivid enough without requiring the stimulation of even so much as a ginger-beer shandy.

be taken into care,' the Almoner went on.

Oh but I would. Yes indeed, then I could go to Vienna and wander the streets till I found him.

The Almoner wanted to inform me that Veritas was to be sent home over Christmas. 'We believe it is important she should spend this precious time with her children. We'll make sure the district nurse comes in every day.'

Veritas definitely perked up. She asked me to bring her some shopping catalogues so she could choose presents.

'From Fortnum and Mason's,' she said. 'You know, that shop in Piccadilly. And one from Harrod's. And that toy shop in Regent Street.'

She wanted catalogues from the most expensive shops in London.

When Denise returned from New York, she was thrilled with her new role and promptly paid a dramatic visit to her new next-of-kin, wearing white leather boots with cut-away toes and a strange conical hat that made her look like an alien.

'Courrèges, darlings,' she told anybody who would listen. 'Isn't he divine? I thought it'd cheer up the nurses if I dressed with flair.'

After she'd shrieked round Veritas's bed and plumped up the pillows, she took me aside.

'But honey sweetheart,' she said in a stage whisper, 'she looks simply ghastly! Why ever didn't you get in touch? And this paupers' hospital! How can she bear it? And in a public ward! No wonder she's not getting better. Never mind, I know of a first-rate faith healer in Harley Street. He treats some of the best people. He did wonders for me.'

Being my mother's next-of-kin seemed to give her the right to drop round to the mews at any time to tell me how to do things I'd been doing on my own for weeks.

'If you need anything, Ruth honey, just call. I'm always at my best in a crisis. And the bins, darling child. A drop of Jeyes Fluid wouldn't come amiss. You do know what Jeyes is?'

Meanwhile, Veritas browsed dreamily through the pages of glossy catalogues. She marked off luxury gifts which were beyond our means.

Denise said, 'If it's helping the poor treasure to stay alive, then it's worth every penny.'

After Veritas had made her selection, I trudged up and down the Portobello Road market, finding substitutes which I wrapped in glittery paper.

Felicity saw through the deception. She found the toy shop catalogue in the string shopping bag. She saw the picture of the gift of her dreams marked with a pencilled *F*: a miniature pony made from leather with a hair mane and removable saddle and harness. Nineteen and a half guineas. In the same bag, she found the brown plastic horse I'd bought from a bric-à-brac stall.

'It's all right,' she told me. 'I'll make myself forget and I'll be surprised on Christmas Day.'

An hour later she said wistfully, 'I'm still trying to forget about the dear little pony. I can't seem to manage.'

I said, 'At least you know Mum knows what you'd really like, even though you can't have it.'

She said, 'When she dies, even the best pony in the world won't be much use, will it? I'd rather have her.'

'Yes, so would I.'

The real winter began. The snow fell. The water pipes froze. The wind whistled through the hardboard walls of the flat. The National Grid couldn't keep up with demand for electricity. So the voltage was erratic, sometimes cut off altogether. If only we lived in a small Sussex hamlet, we could've sent Alfred George out to gather winter fuel where the snow lay dinted.

Mary returned from the Midlands on Christmas Eve. When she discovered how cold the flat was she tried to persuade Veritas to stay in her warm hospital bed.

'But it won't be the same if I'm not with you,' Veritas said. The condemned prisoner's final request had to be granted. The journey home in the ambulance, weaving through the happy throngs of shoppers, exhausted her.

I bought a tin of fruit salad and a boiling fowl. I stuffed it with Paxo to fool them they were eating turkey. All Veritas wanted was milky jelly.

'And she wants it now!' Felicity called from our mother's bed side. Mary stood the jelly mould outside in the sooty snow to make it set faster.

When the electricity fluttered and faded, we heaped dressing-gowns, rugs, cardigans, the old fur coat on top of Veritas. It seemed as though it was only the constant coming and going and heavy breathing of the district nurse with her syringes, swabs and clanking kidney dishes that kept all five of us from freezing to death.

FIFTEEN

Love Is A Many-Splendoured Thing

But she didn't die. Very, very slowly, she began to get better. By the time the scarlet tulips were blooming in the park, she was well enough to totter about the kitchenette creating weird meals for her cookery column. By the time Mary was getting married in the autumn, she was well enough to be writing her cookery column, and a pageant, and had strength enough to make a dress for Mary out of some lace curtains, and a hat for herself which looked like a beehive.

Soon after, the man with blue eyes came back from Vienna. But I was out at an art show with a dreary man called Julius who was more fond of his 1937 Mark 8 Bugatti than he ever would be of me.

But all was not lost, for one fine evening a few weeks later, we met by chance at his friend Harry's place. We seemed pleased to see one another again, but soon started an argument which became so intense that we quite forgot about the other Harry whose party we were at.

We met again next day and seemed to be pleased to see

each other. But when we went out to the cinema, we had a row about the film. He went away to study in Germany. I refused to say goodbye.

I changed my mind. I took a taxi to Victoria Continental Departures but was too late. The boat train had left.

I went to Munich to see him. We could have had a lovely time but we argued about the colour of the sky and about the shape of the moon. We disagreed about the most significant painting in the world, about our least favourite poem, about the origin of the world, the shape of things to come.

I came back to London by rail. He followed, hitchhiking, arrived ahead of me and was there to meet me off the train.

We argued.

We couldn't be quiet together. No more could we be apart.

Mary said, 'Yes, that sounds like love.'

I went to visit my grandmother in her Old People's Home. She remembered who I was, even though I was told she wouldn't.

She said, 'That was a charming young man you brought to see me last summer, Ruth darling. Are you still walking out?'

'Am I what?'

'Is he your beau?'

'I'm not sure,' I said. 'He's in Vienna at the moment.'

'Ah, Vienna. I believe my mama took me there.'

'How can you tell if it's the right one?'

'Oh, I believe you'll know sure enough when it is.'

And it was. So Mary was right. My grandmother was right too. And Veritas too, in her way, was right.

The next time we met, we realised that, since our differences were so complex, our shared interests so many, our arguments so long and confusing, it would take several lifetimes of heated discussion, of sulks, of kisses and reconciliations, even to begin to understand how the other one ticked.

'So we might as well start straight away,' said Harry, putting his big strong hairy arms round me.

I agreed. The other Harry was slightly miffed but cheered up when we asked him to be Best Man.

We married.

We went camping in Shropshire. It rained every day, soft, warm summery rain. Early each morning, inside the damp green tent, while he slept quietly in the sleeping-bag beside me, I wrote him my autobiography so he'd know who I was. And when he surfaced out of sleep, he told me about his dreams for the future (which became my dreams for our future).

We finished our week's wet honeymoon. We began our new life together.

And we lived happily for many years to come.

The End.

THOSE WERE THE DAYS, MY LOVE

SIXTEEN

The Holy Mystery

Our first child was a daughter. She was born in West Africa in a house which had a rusty tin roof and a floor of red beaten earth which was as hard and shiny as lino. All around was green rainforest.

When I heard the baby's first cry of life, I thought it was one of the monkeys playing in the trees outside. Mrs Oguniyi, the midwife who delivered her, called her Sunday because that was the day of her birth. So did the nightwatchman who sat on his straw mat guarding the compound.

'So she is fortunate to have arrived at the best time of the week, even though she is only a girl,' said Mrs Oguniyi with a beaming smile of approval.

Later Harry said to me, 'Just imagine if she'd been born three days earlier on a Thursday!'

I said, 'Do you think Sunday might seem a bit unusual when we go back to Britain? Should we give her a choice of names?'

So in the mission chapel she was baptised both Sunday and Merrily. And when we came back from West Africa, somewhere over the Sahara, the Sunday got lost. She has been Merrily ever since.

When she was four, Merrily learned to read, almost without trying. She did it all the time.

'How extraordinary!' said Harry, who thought that everything about his daughter was amazingly wonderful. So did I, though in a different way.

'Not at all,' I said.

Harry said, 'But *I* couldn't read till I was at least seven.'

'I expect it's hereditary,' I said. 'I was only four when I learned to read. It was as easy as pie.'

By the time she was eight, Merrily had read her way through most of the children's library. But then, when she was twelve, she gave up reading, dyed her hair green, spiked it, and became a Punk. When she was thirteen she dyed her hair black, let it hang over her face, and became a Goth. When she was fourteen she fell in love with another Goth who was incubating chickenpox. (Only the spots hadn't started so he didn't yet know.)

Soon, Merrily got chickenpox too. She lay on the futon in our living room, her face and body white with calamine lotion. She looked like a painted New Guinean dancer. For a while, she couldn't be a Punk or a Goth or even a schoolgirl. She just had to stay there feeling wretched and waiting for the spots to stop itching.

Out of boredom, she began to read again, anything that

was within reach of the futon – Chinese cookery books, shopping catalogues, computer manuals, her father's journals about Third World development, double-glazing leaflets, a craft book called *Patchwork Quilting*. Eventually she found the fading, mildewed pages of the story I'd written for Harry on our honeymoon. For years, ever since our last house-move, it had been squashed down the back of the futon mattress.

'What's this?' she asked.

'It was supposed to be the story of my life,' I said and laughed because I felt embarrassed. 'I wrote it for your dad, years ago.'

'Did Dad like it?'

'I'm not sure. He believes the future is more important than the past.'

'So it's about the olden days?' Merrily asked.

'You could say,' I said.

She hadn't lost her knack of speed-reading. In the time it took me to fetch her youngest brother from school, she'd got to the end, or what I remembered as the end.

'But Mum!' she said. 'It's not finished.'

'Yes it is.'

'But *I'm* not in it.'

'Yes you are.'

'Not properly.'

'You're the gleam in Dad's eye.'

'And you've made our granny seem *quite* different from how she really is.'

141

'She *was* different,' I said, 'back then.'

'Really?' said Merrily with a disbelieving glare. 'And another thing, Grandpa Piers isn't in it at all. He'll be very sad to be left out. He'll think you don't love him. You should write him in and the rest of it.'

'Very well,' I said. 'One of these days I might.'

So, eventually, I did.

And this was what I wrote:

Once, not so long ago, there dwelt in a mean abode above a lock-up garage, a poor widow. Her only son, the apple of her eye, had left home to seek his fortune. Having journeyed to the green and pleasant county of Sussex, he found himself honest labour as a farmhand. He drove Mr Bluefinch's tractor with precision, he milked Mr Bluefinch's cows with gusto, and he rejoiced that he had found his calling so early in life. He was housed by his employer in a modest but adequate one-roomed bothy.

The widow's two elder daughters had found themselves highly satisfactorily life companions and produced two dependents apiece. Her two younger daughters remained faithfully at her side. But they, too, grew restless and eager for the taste of love.

I knew the truth of this for the widow was my mother and the spinsters were my kid sisters.

I knew, too, from lived experience, that a happy marriage is as contagious as the flu. Mary's wedding was followed hard upon by my own.

Blanche was next to catch it. Suddenly, she was leaving school to marry her boyfriend whose name was Zak.

'And if Mum won't let uth,' she said defiantly, 'we'll wun away to Gwetna Gween.'

Seventeen seemed absurdly young.

I said, 'Can't you wait till you're twenty-one?'

'*You* didn't! An' twenty-one'th yearth and yearth away. We're in love now!'

'Why not at least take your A-levels first, like a sensible girl?'

'*You* didn't.'

Our Aunt Speranza, whose own daughter, Faith, was sensibly attending Miss Clara's Chelsea Finishing School where she learned how to arrange flowers, have doors opened for her and get in and out of cars without revealing her stocking-tops, made a special trip, accompanied by our Aunt Thrift, to warn Veritas of the dangers of such young love.

'It's sheer infatuation the girl's got. You'd be mad, Vee, to give your consent. In two months, she'll change her mind. And then she'll be dragging herself through the divorce courts.'

Veritas replied, 'We don't believe in divorce in this family.'

Aunt Thrift gave a sour sniff to add her own endorsement to Aunt Speranza's general disapproval.

'It's only because of what happened to You-Know-Who that they're flinging themselves at any man who passes.'

How dare they insult true love!

My own love was true. It was going to last for a thousand years. Choosing Harry – or being chosen by him, whichever way round it was – was the best thing to have happened to me in my whole life. So might it not be the same for Blanche and Zak? And if, as Aunt Speranza implied, it was because we were fatherless waifs that we sought love so early, what was wrong with that?

Zak seemed a nice enough person, though he seldom spoke. Perhaps it was the quantity of women inspecting him like livestock that frightened him into silence.

Aunt Speranza said, 'And why must Vee's girls choose so *improvidently*? Why won't any of them find a chap with a job?'

Aunt Thrift said, 'They take after Vee. She married You-Know-Who without a brass farthing to his name. And look what became of that!'

Zak was a long-haired design student. He wore a sad, droopy moustache, a tight headband low on his brow and round, pink-lensed glasses. So many adornments gave his head a busy look even when he was sitting quite still meditating, which he did several times a day to the sound of a record of Indian sitar music.

Blanche showed off her left hand with a large ornament on the ring finger which caught the light more like a massive chunk of ice than a diamond.

'Ith perthpecth,' Blanche said proudly. 'Thak made it for me in hith college workthop.'

'It's what?' I said.

'Perspex, man,' said Zak. 'Cool.'

'A plastic engagement ring?' said Aunt Speranza. 'How perfectly extraordinary. What will they think of next!'

'The new way, man. Whole world's gonna go plastic, man. Kettles, cars, spaceships.' This was Zak's longest sentence ever. 'Kinda cool. Like.'

It was to be a kinda cool wedding too. Kinda hip.

On her wedding morning, Mary and little Stella took a bowl of Rice Krispies to Blanche in the top bunk, to make her feel special.

'Bridal breakfast,' said Mary, and Stella scrambled up the bunk-bed ladder and under the blankets beside her young aunt.

Blanche didn't seem pleased with the attention. She got up and wandered round the flat, naked except for the perspex ring. Her auburn ringlets curled softly down to her freckled shoulders.

'Isn't she looking pretty?' said Veritas fondly. 'If only Father could see her.'

I wasn't too sure. If he came back now, he'd find the world too changed. He wouldn't recognise any of us. As for Blanche, I thought she'd look a lot prettier if she hadn't decided to be in such a bad mood today.

'Can't find any clean knickerth!' she snarled. 'Whooth thtolen them? I bet ith Felithity. Thee's alwayth taking my thingth. Thith ith the latht time thee'll ever do it!'

'Only wedding nerves,' said Mary calmly. 'A good sign. Everybody has them.'

I didn't remember that I had. I'd remembered being happy all day.

'Ith only becoth I had to thleep here, without Thak, an I'm mithing him. Mum thaid I had to. Ith bad luck to thleep under the thame roof the night before you mawwy.'

'You mean you usually sleep with him? You've already moved in with him?'

'Yeth. He uthed to make thure I got to thchool in time. Mum never did.'

'Gosh,' I said, quite shocked.

So was Mary ten minutes later when Blanche had had her turn in the black marble bathroom.

'Oh no!' gasped Mary. 'What *has* she done to her hair?'

Where there had been auburn curls, now the top of Blanche's head was as stubbly as a bathbrush.

'Ith a fringe,' Blanche said. 'I juth cut it.'

'She should never have been left alone,' Mary said. 'What will poor Zak say when he sees?'

'He won't mind. He'll only be looking at her inner beauty.'

'We mustn't let Mum see. She'll be very upset.'

Felicity had been weaving a headdress out of plane-tree leaves with twists of ivy. It was as untidy as a rook's nest and as large as a wreath laid for the unknown soldier at the Cenotaph. Felicity said, 'She'll be fine once she's got this on.'

'Will she?' I said. I certainly wouldn't have wanted to stand at the altar with a rook's nest on my head.

But strangely, she was. She seemed genuinely pleased and thanked Felicity with a hug. I could see that sisters were complex and peculiar creatures. I felt glad to be a wife and mother too.

The remainder of Blanche's bridal outfit was a cloud of floating silk scarves, semi-stitched together, though no shoes and still no knickers.

'She mustn't go to church without knickers,' I said. 'Should she, Mary? *You* tell her. She listens to what you say.'

But Mary didn't think it mattered. 'Medieval ladies didn't wear knickers, and that's what she's trying to look like, isn't she? I think you're worrying about the wrong things, Ruth.'

Blanche wasn't wearing a bra under the scarves either.

'Of course not,' said Felicity. 'Nobody does any more. They're a symbol of male repression.'

Zak was not the repressing type. At the church we found him leaning against the railings having a relaxed chat with Alfred George who was, as usual for his sisters' marriages, wearing our father's morning suit though it still didn't quite fit him. Zak was wearing a new headband, beaded, and an embroidered tent-dress.

'Thnot a dreth. Ith a kaftan,' Blanche explained.

Their friends were also beaded, headbanded, bangled and kaftanned. The bright swirly colours outdazzled the pastel floral silks of the traditional female guests. There were a great many of both types, beaded and softly floral. Just because the aunts considered Blanche too young to know her own mind, was no reason for denying her as good a send-off as could be created for ten pounds.

'But Veritas, sweetheart!' gasped Denise, arriving by taxi at the last moment, hatted and dressed by Dior. 'You should have warned me it was going to be a hippy thing. I'd have tried to blend in!'

Denise would never blend.

Veritas said, 'Everybody's having their weddings like this these days. Even the Royals. It's the new way.'

After church, we carried a picnic party to the park.

When the multi-coloured cake (created by Veritas from everything she could find at the back of the store cupboard) had been ceremonially cut with a penknife, and the festal sweetmeats (that were mostly toast fingers with a scrape of Shrimpton's fishpaste), and the wine cup (that was mostly Kia-Ora fruit squash enlivened with drops of rum essence) had been eaten and drunk, the party was over. The park gates closed at dusk. The traditional guests left. But the beaded and bearded ones wouldn't go away. They mooched in their psychedelic groups towards the mews and up the concrete fire-steps to the flat. When there was no standing space left inside, guests climbed on to the bunk-bed and up through the skylight on to the roof-valley.

The partying continued amongst the pigeons and chimney pots. When there was no food or drink left, the night-music began. Guests had guitars and finger-cymbals and tabla and plastic flutes. One curly-headed boy in patchwork flares brought a guitar on his back and a string hammock on his shoulder which he slung between two chimney stacks. He was soon stretched comfortably out and strumming along with the rest.

Candles in jamjars were lit and joss sticks were gently smouldering.

Mary and I tucked our sleepy tots into the lower bunk-bed and joined the roof party.

Veritas was already up there, sitting on a cushion. Zak had brought her up a pint of beer.

'Your mam, she's just so cool, man,' he said.

The wedding party went on till the clatter of the first Underground train at five. And the influenza of love was spreading more quickly than anyone might have guessed.

SEVENTEEN

Just Puppy Love

By morning, Felicity had a smiling and contented look about her as though her brain had been removed and replaced with pink candy floss. She was still up on the roof, lying in Curly Top's hammock. They were one each end, gazing dumbstruck at one another as they swayed gently in the dawn breeze.

'She wouldn't even come down for breakfast,' I said. 'I was wondering if they might like a mug of tea taken up. Or would that be interfering?'

'Yes,' said Mary. 'It would.'

Veritas said, 'Aah, just puppy love!'

But it wasn't. According to Felicity when she came down from the roof, it was the real thing. And she'd rescheduled her future accordingly.

So when Blanche began packing her possessions into a rucksack ready to leave home with her Zak, so did Felicity, ready to leave with her Curly Top.

'Please don't keep calling him Curly Top. His name's Ace.'

'And where are you going?'

'Across the Channel. Ace has been left a farm in France. We're going to reclaim his inheritance and grow sunflowers together for the rest of our lives.'

'Sunflowers? What for?'

'To sell.'

'You mean for chicken feed?'

'No, as flowers, to flower shops.'

'I've never seen sunflowers for sale in a florist. They sell things like roses and lilies.'

'Not yet you haven't. But you will. Just you wait and see.'

'Really, Felicity! Be sensible,' I told my sister. 'You're not a business woman, you're a schoolgirl. You've got to do your O-levels. You can't go rushing off to France.'

'You and Mary did. Nobody stopped *you*.'

'Things were different then. It was the olden days. The world was safer. And anyway, we didn't rush off with the first boy we met. We went with each other.'

'Ace isn't the first boy I've met. He's the first person I've properly fallen in love with. And he's the last. We're going to stay together and grow sunflowers for the rest of our lives.'

Under her pale calm, Felicity was as determined as any of us. Perhaps more so. That was the advantage of being the youngest. She'd got to grow up fastest. She'd been able to pick up tips from observing the rest of us.

Ace was still stretched out in his hammock. He looked like a sweetly lovable puppy. But how good would he be at tilling the stony soil under the hot sun?

I said, 'Listen, Felicity, if you're determined to go, don't you think you ought to get married first, rather than live in sin?'

'Oh really, Ruthie! You're so old-fashioned! Nobody gets married these days. Not just because of living together.'

I said, 'Blanche just has. Is *she* old-fashioned?'

'She's probably pregnant. That's the only reason anybody gets married these days.'

The world was changing fast. My sisters had a different outlook. I said, 'What about Mum? Doesn't she mind?'

'No. It's her idea. She says she's tired of all this getting married that everybody's doing. First Mary, then you, now Blanche. Even Alfred George looks as though he's heading that way. Look at that dreamy girl who keeps trailing after him.'

Mary said, 'So what are we going to do about Veritas? Now that Felicity's leaving as well, she's going to be on her own.'

All those years she'd spent bringing us up, if not well, at any rate as well as she was capable. Now the mothering was suddenly over. She was going to be on her own. She never liked being left behind. She liked to be the one who led the way to new places.

I said, 'Perhaps she'll go to Tunis.'

Blanche said, 'Why would thee want to do that?'

'On foggy days when we all had coughs and colds, Father used to say that's where they'd move to. After he died, she still went on about a Bedouin tent on the edge of an oasis.'

Felicity said, 'Sounds fab. Then she'll be nearer to me and Ace.'

She couldn't really go to North Africa. There wasn't the money. Even if we had a serious whip-round, we wouldn't collect enough to send her further than Brighton.

Alfred George said, 'She could come and stay with me,' then added, 'I suppose.'

'Or me,' said Blanche. 'But you're her favouwite.'

Alfred George said, 'It wouldn't be much fun for her.'

'Or we could take it in turns to have her?' Mary suggested.

I said, 'I don't know where Harry and I are going to be living next.' And I was sure I didn't want Veritas cooking inedible austerity meals, and cutting up the bedding to sew into summer frocks, and making bookshelves out of wooden orange boxes.

Mary said, 'She'd help you with your babies. That's what grannies are for – light household tasks.'

But we both knew that Veritas had never been talented at the repetitive side of parenting. Making fun out of nothing, good times out of bad, being a merry widow – that's what she was best at.

Blanche said, 'Perhapth thee thould go and live with one of her thithterth.'

'Would *you* want to live with Aunt Speranza and her antimacassars and cork drink-coasters?'

'No.'

Mary said, 'Perhaps she'll be glad we've all left at last? She'll have time to do the things proper people do.'

'Such as?'

'Going to the Bingo hall?'

It sounded unlikely. In the end, Mary asked Veritas directly if she had any plans for the future.

'Plans? Well, yes, I thought I'd start clearing up some of the party mess, then I'd go round the pockets and see if I can find a few shillings, then I'll buy some spaghetti from the corner shop and cook up a pan of pasta with this new recipe I've discovered. You add seaweed and old breadcrumbs. So at least I'll know you're all properly fed before you set off on your journeys.'

I said, 'Mary meant, later. After we've left.'

'Oh that!' Veritas tossed the concept aside. 'You know, Ruth, when you've survived two world wars, and when your darling husband has died, and when you've been told you've only got three months left to live, worrying about the tomorrows doesn't seem terribly important. However, since you ask, I've got to finish my new pageant. It's set in a soup kitchen. And I've said I'll help out with the Brownies' Harvest Pageant. Then I'll sort out my frocks and see if I can sew some smocks for my grandchildren. Do children still wear smocks? Then it'll be nearly Christmas, so I'll ice a cake and mix up some mincemeat, and I'll start to get ready for you all to come and stay. You *will* all come, won't you, darlings? I'm sure we'll fit in somehow.'

It sounded almost convincing. She wasn't going to pine

with loneliness. She was going to settle down to being a grandmother.

We helped clear up the debris of the party. We ate the seaweed pasta. Then we went away and got on with our other lives and occasionally thought of Veritas sewing smocks out of frocks and writing pageants and helping the Brownies in the community hall.

And none of us had a clue about what she was really going to do with the rest of her life. Nor had she until it hit her with the impact of a loose boulder tumbling down from the summit of a very high mountain crag.

EIGHTEEN

La Vie en Rose

We were like seed-fluff from the dandelion, once growing side by side on our shared stalk, now scattered on the wind to the corners of the earth.

Felicity was farming sunflowers in Provence, Mary was in Canada, Blanche in a Welsh commune, Alfred George farming for Mr Bluefinch.

Since I'd chosen Harry, for richer for poorer, for better for worse, for nearer for further, my own corner was currently Aberdeen, the most northerly city of the British Isles, further north even than Moscow. In Aberdeen, it rained every day and, once autumn arrived, it never got light.

We shared our tenement flat with a Texan teacher, an Israeli violinist and a French drama student.

Veritas wrote often, not letters so much as curiosities. She sent funny dollies she'd made out of paper for Merrily. She sent our second child, a boy we called Peregrine, a fabric book with pocket pages she'd made out of an old curtain and a floral dirndl. She sent a handful of freshly-picked blackberries. At least, they had once been. By the time they arrived, they'd turned into an envelopeful of purple juice. I could just about read her scrawled and juice-stained note.

'*Found these growing by the railway siding. They're going to create a city farm for children, whatever that is.*'

Sometimes, she sent new manuscripts for me to copy-type. That was a good sign. It meant she was keeping on keeping on.

So, though we were far apart in miles, we kept in touch.

Then an obscure message arrived which I didn't understand. When I opened the envelope, a shower of rose petals fluttered out. They caried a distant fragrance which dimly reminded me of my grandmother's long-ago garden.

Veritas had sent some peculiar items, but never before loose petals. Nothing else. No letter. No card. What was going on? Was she missing her children so much she couldn't bear to write?

I pushed through the soft Scottish drizzle to take Merrily and Peregrine to Toddler Group in a chilly hall. On the way, on impulse, I dived into the telephone kiosk, leaving the tots in the rain in the pushchair. They were used to it. I dialled my mother's number. Long-distance trunk call. An absurd expense. Ten shillings at least. But I had to find out. Was she all right? The number rang and rang.

At the end of Toddler Group, it was still drizzling. I tried again. I had all the shillings with me that were meant to go in the gas meter. Still no reply.

So I pushed on towards the port to buy mackerel from the quayside. One and elevenpence a pound. The rain in Aberdeen was wet. The winter days were dark. But the fish was fresh and plentiful. As was my love for Harry.

I bought a magazine too: *Young Miss Petticoat.* I was going to try my hand at writing stories again. I felt I had so much to say about our time in West Africa, though as I read about the fashion of the young misses, I felt a million years old. Mini-skirts were going out. Dollyrockers were coming in. I hadn't even known what a Dollyrocker was till I saw a picture of a skimpy flowery shift with puff sleeves. I was twenty-three and out-of-touch.

By the afternoon post, another strange envelope. This time, no petals, no blackberry pulp but an explanatory letter (of sorts).

'*Darling darling darling, Ruthie,*' she began. So many darlings! This was unusually effusive.

'*Isn't life strange and wonderful? Never have the trees looked so lovely. Never has birdsong sounded so sweet. There is a blackbird that perches on the windowsill every morning and looks in at me.*'

Was this part of a new pageant?

No.

Was she getting ready to join Blanche's hippy commune?

No.

Was she into her second childhood?

Perhaps.

When Veritas wrote, '*And there was such a brilliant sunset last evening, casting a glow over everything,'* she sounded like a dizzy schoolgirl. I could remember going goo-goo over sunsets. She ended her letter,

'*Longing to talk to you. Soon be Christmas. Love to you and your darling babies.'*

What was she on about? Sunsets, flowers, making friends with blackbirds, never needing to sleep – her letter wasn't actually about anything.

Almost before I'd finished reading it, the phone was ringing in the communal hall downstairs. She never rang in daytime. Usually she didn't ring at all. Unless there was bad news. Like when my grandmother was dying. But I knew it was her. The timbre of the tone.

'Hello, darling. All well?' Her long-distance voice was echoey. I could almost see the hundreds of miles of the A1 trunk-road between us.

Once again, she had nothing to say, except to tell me how lovely the leaves on the trees in the park were.

Bizarre.

She was the weirdest mother. Harry's wasn't like that. She communicated via sensible five-shilling book tokens and hand-knitted socks with properly turned heels. I loved both Harry's mother and my own, but in such different ways.

'It's part of the deal, isn't it?' said Harry. 'Loving your lover, you need to love your lover's mother too.'

'Yes, Harry,' I said. I'd never thought of it like that.

I loved him for his placid wisdom. If only I could've met

159

him sooner, say when I was ten, then I could have bypassed all the bad bits of my life.

'What bad bits?'

'When I didn't love my mother. When I missed my father.'

If only. If only things had been different. But then if things had been too different, I might never have met him.

NINETEEN

A Whole Lotta Shakin' Going On

The next time I saw my sisters was at a memorial service. It was for our grandmother. Not a sad occasion.

As Uncle Guillemot said from the pulpit, 'A thanksgiving to celebrate her long and active life.'

There was some rousing hymn-singing, and a jostle of jolly cousins for us to catch up with. I thought it made a good change for Veritas too, to break the tedium of her lonely life.

'Lonely!' said Blanche. 'You muth be joking! Thee's never in. I tried to call her thimply loaths of timeth. I wanted her to be the firtht to have my newth.'

Blanche's face, usually so robustly pink, was as white as her name, the very pallor that Mary and I had endeavoured to create when we used to go Up the Caves. Only Blanche wasn't wearing make-up. It was natural.

'Ith early morning thickneth,' she said. 'Exthept ith all day long.'

She was pregnant. So was Felicity. They both seemed

proud of themselves.

They'd hitchhiked to St Augustine's Church directly from a Ban the Bomb protest.

'We marched all round the air base,' said Felicity. 'It was miles. And there were hundreds of people and loads of police dogs.'

Mother-hennish, I said, 'Is it good for your babies to go on demos?'

'Exthremely good,' said Blanche, stroking her tummy fondly.

'It'll be much worse for them if we don't,' said Felicity.

'We have to thave the world for them, and for your children and for all future generationth.'

When Mary and I had gone hitching, it was more to see how far we could go than to save anything. I was impressed.

Felicity had abandoned the sunflower project. And Ace.

'Why? I thought you were in love?'

'We are. But our stars aren't in alignment. We should've checked it out. Never mind, I know he'll find someone else much more suitable.'

'But what about *you*?' My poor little baby sister, unmarried, pregnant, alone. It was worrying.

'Course I'm not alone! I've got all my family, haven't I? I'm going to live at Blanchie's commune. We'll have a green birthing and share bringing up the babies.'

'Tho they'll be more like twinth than couthinth.'

Veritas was sitting in a pew at the front of the church

with her sisters and brothers. I didn't see her at first. Her face was hidden beneath an odd black thing like an upturned waste-paper basket. It was supposed to be a high-fashion hat. She'd clearly made it herself.

I thought, Aha, now that she's got time for millinery, she's got time to have Merrily and Peregrine for a couple of nights so Harry and I can go off with the tent.

It was the wrong think to have.

Blanche said, 'Thee won't have time. Thee thays thee's in love.'

How could she be? She was four times a grandmother, and another two on the way.

'She *thinks* she's in love,' Mary, wisely cautious, corrected her.

So that's what all those rose petals and crazy messages were about! Not senility, but the derangement of emotional disturbance.

Felicity whispered, 'If you look quickly over your shoulder you can see him. He's here.'

'Which one?'

'Near the back. Behind the font, came in at the last moment.'

I saw a tall elderly man with thick white hair. He was leaning on a silver-headed cane. He had a blue spotted silk hanky sticking out of his top pocket. He looked discreetly distinguished rather than handsome.

'Are we meant to know?'

'She keeps dropping hints, then going pink and flustery.'

'But Alfred George's met him. He was summoned to London.'

'Why him?'

'Because he's the male of the species, of course. He said he had to sit in the old man's library and drink dry sherry which tasted like turpentine. He said he's terribly posh and he's got a title.'

'Like a lord?'

'Not exactly. More of a sir. His name's Piers.'

I'd never heard of anyone called Piers before apart from a medieval ploughman. 'Where'd she find him?'

'She says the angels sent him. It's fate, her destiny. Something about smoke gets in your eyes.'

How odd. I couldn't remember that she used to believe in fairy nonsense. It was irritating that Alfred George knew about it first. I said, snappily, 'How long's it been going on?' I could hear my voice beginning to sound like Aunt Speranza's.

'After Blanchie's wedding. He'd noticed it. He'd been driving past and thought it was a fancy dress party. The next day, she went back to the church to make sure the flowers were cleared up. He happened to be there so he helped her. He claimed he was sightseeing, looking at the stained glass windows. Anyway, he gave her a lift back to the flat and then she invited him in for supper.'

'That was terribly forward of her.'

'Only she found there wasn't anything to give him. So

he took her to the Ritz because it's the only place he knows.'

Blanche said, 'And they had oythters and thampagne, and woatht quailth.'

Aphrodisiac food! The rotter! The bounder!

'I suppose she thinks if you get picked up by a strange man inside a church it's all right?'

Mary said, 'She's been to stay with him too.'

Outrageous! 'Without even taking a chaperone?'

It sounded as though she'd already broken every one of her own rules of conduct.

'It's all right. She wasn't ever alone with him. It was a house-party at his country house. His housekeeper was there, and his valet. There's a butler too. And a chauffeur. He's got a place in Italy too. A villa where he can go in the summertime.'

'Blimey!' I was gobsmacked, not just the wealth, but as much because I didn't know that old people could fall in love. I said, 'Perhaps it's only puppy love.'

Alfred George didn't think so.

I said, 'So if it's serious, did you ask him if his intentions were honourable?'

Of course he hadn't.

I said, 'We don't want her being hurt, or left in the lurch, or anything like that. We ought to find out what his future plans are.'

Alfred George said, 'Does it really matter?'

'Yes.'

He said, 'It's up to her what she gets up to.'

'No it isn't. She's our mother. It's up to us.'

And since Alfred George wouldn't go and ask him, Mary and I had to. We had to run to catch up with him. He obviously wasn't intending to come and eat Bath buns in the church hall with the rest of the congregation. A sleek black car was waiting beyond the lych gate. A chauffeur in a sleek suit was holding the door open.

I nudged Mary forward. But suddenly, she went dumb.

So I said very fast, 'Excuse me, Sir Piers, but we are Veritas's senior daughters. And in a matriarchal family such as ours, it is the custom to ask the eldest daughter's permission before you go gallivanting out with the figurehead. So we hope your intentions are entirely honourable and that you intend to give her a good time. Well, at least, don't make her unhappy whatever you do because she's had enough of that for a lifetime. And she may seem a bit daft sometimes and wear stupid home-made hats but that's the way she's always been. I hope I make myself clear?'

He was about to reply, but Mary pulled me away. 'You've said quite enough,' she hissed. 'I think he's got the point.'

We belted back to the safety of the church hall where Blanche and Felicity were stuffing themselves with buns as though they hadn't eaten in days.

They were going to need someone to advise them about a sensible diet during pregnancy.

Felicity said, 'By the way, I've checked out their star signs and everything's perfectly in alignment.'

So Venus was definitely in the ascendant. Perhaps I needn't have bothered with accosting Sir Piers.

In Aberdeen it was raining. Veritas was ringing me almost before I got back. Another of her high-cost trunk-calls. I was pounding nappies in the stone sink and wondering, Can I get one dry before Peregrine wakes from his nap? I was remembering living in West Africa. Nappies dried there in twenty minutes.

'Hello, Ruth. You busy?'

'No, Mum. Just the usual. Nappies.'

'I've got some news. I don't know how you'll take it.'

So was this going to be good news or bad?

'He's asked me to marry him.'

Aha! I thought. So my speech has borne fruit. I said, 'And what did you say?'

But she hardly needed to tell me. Even from four hundred and ninety-two miles away I could hear that she was smiling. It made me smile.

Not puppy love. Granny love.

TWENTY

To Have And To Hold

We met up for Blanche and Felicity's babies' triple christening. (Felicity's baby turned out to be twins. That's probably why she was hungry for buns at our grandmother's memorial.) Veritas was wearing the fly-net hat she'd made for my wedding. It hadn't caught any flies, but it looked very dusty.

Sir Piers came too, but separately. He brought an ivory and silver teething ring for each of the new babies. He didn't touch the babies or get near them, but nor did he turn away in disgust.

I didn't expect to like him. You're not supposed to like your stepfather.

Mary said, 'You're thinking of step*mothers*. But Alfred George's right. It doesn't really matter what we think. The important thing is, d'you think he *really* loves her?'

'Why shouldn't he?'

'He's so posh.'

I said, 'Mum's posh too, in her own way. She's always been keen on dukes and earls. She got it from Father. And she knows the rules about when to wear gloves, and how to peel a dessert pear, and about not speaking to the Queen unless she speaks to you first.'

'He might be too rich for her.'

'Actually,' said Blanche, 'ith eathier for wich people to fall in love becauth they haven't got to wathte tho much energy thwimming.'

'Swimming?'

'You know,' Blanche explained. 'That thing Mum'th alwayth gone on about when there wathn't any money. Keeping our headth above water.'

'Oh! Not swimming. You mean, riding with the tide.'

Veritas was certainly doing that.

'I only hope she's going to manage all right,' I said.

Blanche thought I meant Felicity. 'Thee's got mathes of milk for both of them,' she said.

I meant Veritas. My earlier confidence was beginning to wane. Blanche said, 'So whath thee got to manage?'

'Having everything perfect, no muddles, no messes. It might be difficult getting used to it.'

'It'll be wonderful,' said Felicity. 'She won't have to do anything ever again, not even cook his breakfast.'

'Unleth thee's feeling all lovey-dovey and wanth to coddle him an egg,' said Blanche, who was obviously still feeling lovey-dovey about Zak.

'Or do her own ironing,' added Felicity. (Not that any of

us could remember ever having seen our mother do any ironing.)

'Thee hathn't got to earn her own living.'

'She'll be a kept woman!'

Our grandmother used to say that a kept woman was indescribably wicked, nearly as bad as the man who kept her.

'No she won't. She'll be like a proper, normal wife.'

There was to be no baling out. He'd set the date.

So it was that Mary, Blanche, Felicity and I travelled from our various corners of the earth to converge on the mews flat. We brought our offspring and our sleeping bags.

Sir Piers wanted a quiet occasion, or so he said. No confetti, no bridesmaids, no child pages in velvet breeches. He hadn't even announced his forthcoming marriage in *The Times*.

Blanche said, 'I'm thure Mum'd wather have a noithy kneeth-up.'

Mary said, 'Perhaps he's ashamed of her and doesn't want anybody to see.'

Hardly surprising, I thought, if she insists on making herself such peculiar headgear.

They'd told only us and Sir Piers's two nieces who were nearly as old as him.

'Quite doddery, both of them,' Veritas said. 'But simply thrilled to bits. I think they were hoping to be bridesmaids.'

Nobody else was informed, but people found out anyway. Most had an opinion.

'It'll never work,' Cousin Roland (who wasn't really a cousin, and who'd had his own eye on Veritas for years) rang up to tell Mary. 'You wouldn't want to throw away everything just for a short time of fun.'

But what had she got to throw away? A dingy flat that was due for demolition.

Denise agreed with Roland. She didn't just ring, she called round with a bottle of gin as a bribe.

'You're crazy, Veritas,' she said. 'If he's not been married by his age, he's clearly a confirmed bachelor. I know the type. My second husband was just the same.'

'As a matter of fact, they're heaven-sent for each other,' said Mary, now that she and I and Blanche and Felicity had decided they were.

Denise said, 'How can they be? He's an industrialist and she's a poor widow. They have absolutely nothing in common!'

'They do,' I said. 'They've both worked hard all their lives. The only difference is, he earned himself a knighthood for his efforts. She ought to have one too, but women aren't offered them however much they deserve them.'

Aunt Speranza's opinion was also that it was absurd. 'Flirting at *her* age! She's always been a show-off. She's nearly sixty!'

'No,' I corrected her. 'Only fifty-three. And Winston

Churchill didn't take over the government and start winning the war till he was over sixty.'

'The chap she fancies is as old as the hills, so I've heard,' said Aunt Speranza.

'Oldish,' I agreed, 'but not as the hills. And he's very sprightly. He wears spats and has his moustaches waxed.'

'Our poor mother!' sighed my aunt. 'She'd turn in her grave if she knew.'

'Granny was cremated. Ashes find it even harder to turn than skeletons.'

'Pah!' said Aunt Speranza. 'Just wait till Charité hears. She's going to be deeply disturbed.'

Since the union was inevitable, Denise changed her approach and offered enthusiastic support. She nominated herself a leading role: Matron of Honour. She'd been married four times. She was an expert.

'Derry and Toms! The Bridal Mezzanine!' she said. 'That's where she'll find the perfect gown. We can have a drinky-poo on the roof gardens after.'

Denise had to be restrained. No way was Veritas to shop for clothes on tick. We'd done a whip-round to pay off her last quarter's bills.

'And she's not starting married life in debt.'

'Then perhaps I'll lend her something,' said Denise.

If space-age mini-skirt designer suits, white leather boots with cut away toes, little black cocktail dresses and sequinned evening hats were too youthful for Denise, they were out of the question for the granny-bride.

Even one of Veritas's own bedspread frocks would be more suitable.

'He wants her for herself, not for what she's wearing. Don't worry, Denise, we'll sort her out.'

We started with the beaten egg-white for her face. This was girls' business. We sent our children out to the park to play on the swings with their daddies and their uncle Alfred George while we got to work.

While the egg-white dried, we rootled through the wire hangers on the back of the door. We managed to agree on a flowery cotton frock (former bedroom curtains) less gaudy than the rest. Mary rushed down the road with it to the Whirlpool Launderette. Meanwhile, Blanche went to buy a pair of nylons. She got them cheap from a dodgy man selling from a suitcase on the pavement.

Mary fetched the frock. Felicity ironed it. I blancoed a pair of white sling-backs. They'd already walked down a church aisle twice so they knew the way.

We clubbed together for the seventeen and sixpence for a shampoo and set at the Paragon Salon next to the Whirlpool. She came back with a hot red face, a blue rinse and a tight granny perm.

'I thaid it wath money down the dwain,' said Blanche as we rinsed away the blue and re-set the bridal curls.

Throughout her beauty treatment, the bride-to-be remained as docile as a lamb. When the children came back, little Stella demanded, 'What've you done to my granny? She looks all different. Like Cinderella.'

Veritas gave Stella a hug. 'Today,' she said, 'I *am* Cinderella.'

TWENTY-ONE

From This Day Forth

It was a dark ancient church across the square from Sir Piers' town house. So quiet. No music. No cocktail-party chatter. It smelled of wax polish, stone, and lilies.

Not a single invitation had been sent, yet there were over forty people, all waiting. And all curious. Her seven siblings and their spouses. Two very old churchwardens from St Augustine's where she'd grown up. The Bluefinches, the Hares, Colonel Buckstaff and the publican from The Ploughshare, a theatre impresario who'd known our father, two medics who'd been student lodgers. It was like a brief summary of her life.

We, her descendents, had to take the empty pews near the back. He was definitely here, at the front, in his tail coat and pinstripe trousers, an elderly niece on either side.

There was an expectant hush. Everybody was holding their breath. She was late.

'Can't see!' Merrily called out. 'Can't see my granny! Granny! Where you hiding?'

Nobody laughed. The suspense was almost tangible.

'Ssh! She's not here yet.' Harry lifted Merrily up to stand on the pew for a better view.

And then we heard the scuffle of footsteps in the porch. Uncle Guillemot gave the signal to the organist up in the organ loft. The organ pipes filled with air and burst into music.

She came in on Alfred George's arm, the prayer book in her other hand, quivering. It looked as though he was holding her quite tightly. Slowly, too slowly, they began the walk up the centre of the church. Was she having second thoughts? Was he having to *pull* her towards the altar?

Had she ever before looked demure? The lilies-of-the-valley nestling on her head were trembling slightly. She looked too solemn. I wanted to call out, 'This isn't a funeral, Mum!'

Even chatty Merrily was silenced. She stared with her mouth half open. Peregrine held his blue fluffy elephant on his head so it could see. I thought, If only the grey ashes of her mother could have come out from their buried urn and flown here to witness a wayward daughter's late blossoming! But Granny Ruth hadn't been at Veritas's first wedding either.

I thought, If only the white bones of our father could have struggled up from their grave and danced their way up the A21 to be here. But would he have recognised her as she was now?

The mother of the bride is often said to cry when she

sees her daughter walk to meet her groom. Would it be all right for a daughter of the bride to weep? I felt an ache in my throat and was ready to howl. Harry knew. Without us exchanging a word, his hand found mine and squeezed.

Until she was nearly halfway down the church, she seemed to be walking in a daze. Then she seemed to jolt into reality and see where she was. She glanced at the tense faces. She broke into a broad smile. She almost ran the rest of the way.

I distinctly remembered her reprimand at my marriage. 'Do stop smiling, Ruth,' she'd said. 'You mustn't look eager. It's not dignified.'

But this was her marriage, not mine. She could do it any way she liked.

Alfred George dropped her off at the altar steps and the service began.

Uncle Guillemot got them to the bit where he looked straight into Sir Piers's eyes and Sir Piers looked straight back and Uncle Guillemot had to ask him if he'd 'love her, comfort her, honour and keep her, in sickness and in health?'

I felt light-headed enough to faint as my own heart gave a leap, for these were the same cherished things which Harry had promised, in front of Uncle Guillemot, to do. Then, when Sir Piers said he would, my heart gave another little leap. How very long she'd been without any source of love, comfort, honour, and being kept through sickness and health!

Uncle Guillemot got to the next bit about 'forsaking all others as long as you both shall live'. He hurried them on quickly. Given the bridegroom's age, it wouldn't have done to dwell on the bit about 'till death do you part'.

And then they'd done the bit with the rings and Uncle Guillemot was declaring that they were Man and Wife together.

Thus, according to God's holy ordinance, Veritas had got a husband, we'd got a stepfather, and seven children had gained a grandfather.

We spilled out of the church behind them in a mood of grinning joyfulness. I noticed that even Aunt Speranza, whose purse-string lips were usually tied tight-shut, was smiling.

In the churchyard, a posse of pressmen were jostling with cameras and spiral notebooks to catch the happy couple.

Mary said, 'I thought no one was meant to know?'

'Somebody must have tipped them off.'

I wondered, Was it Sir Piers himself? He paused carefully, with Veritas at his side, and let the cameras flash. Then he held up his hand. He had a statement.

'Thank you, gentlemen. I will be brief. Today is a day of miraculous and bountiful change. Not only have I had the great privilege to marry a wonderful women – ' he paused to give the hacks in macs time to write it down – 'I have also had the superb good fortune to gain a complete and ready-made family so that I may never again be lonely.'

Blanche whispered, 'Bit over the top, ithn't he? He'th

making it thound ath though we're all going to live with him.'

His nieces were near the back of the crowd otherwise they might have resented the implication that, over the years, their uncle had found their company tedious. One of them was being chatted up by Cousin Roland. Old folks flirting on hallowed ground might have struck some people as gruesome. But I'd just witnessed with my own eyes how geriatrics can fall as genuinely in love as the rest of us.

The couple graciously consented to pose for one more round of clicking cameras. Then Sir Piers led the way across the leafy square to his town house. We followed. A journalist trailed after us.

'Excuse us, love. Spare a name or two?' He was like a greedy starling who hadn't got his share of titbits. 'The young lady – the bride – anyone famous, is she?'

'Our mum,' I said.

'Who goes by the name of . . .'

'Veritas.'

'*Lady* Veritath to you,' added Blanche.

The pressman jotted it down. 'Ta, ever so,' he said. 'Household name, is she, ducks?'

'Oh yes,' I said. 'Very.'

'What she do then? Actress, variety show?'

'Something like that.'

Blanche and I caught up with the others going up the steps in our mother's white and elegant new home.

Blanche said, 'Why didn't you tell him Mumth a well-known pageant writer and wireleth perthonality?'

I said, 'Why didn't you?'

Sir Piers must have guessed how many well-wishers there might be. He'd arranged a reception at his house. It was supposed to be informal. It was meticulous, almost as though he'd been practising all his life to get it right.

Mary said, 'Or else his butler has.'

There was proper champagne and plenty of it. The cake was not half a dozen trifle sponges held together with butter icing but a confectioner's masterpiece, in three tiers, with pillars, silvered leaves and white sugar roses. His timing was also a masterpiece. He was old. He didn't want it to drag on too long. They were to dine at the Ritz and leave for Italy next day.

The shiny Daimler, driven by the sleek chauffeur, turned up on cue. Sir Piers and Lady Veritas (who was only a little flushed from excitement) climbed in.

'Goodbye, goodbye, good luck. Goodbye!' we called. We went on waving and watching as the black car slid into the swirl of Hyde Park and away towards Piccadilly.

We went back into our stepfather's house to get our coats and bags. We didn't have to clear up the party. The caterers were already doing it. So we gathered up our pushchairs and babies and children, those of us that already had some, and our husband/boyfriend/girlfriend, and we sauntered off to the tube station.

'So that's the end of all her troubles,' said Felicity with a sigh.

'Yup,' I agreed.

'Probably,' added Mary, who would always be both wise and cautious.

We hugged and kissed one another goodbye before starting our journeys back to our own homes and our own lives. And then we all lived happily ever after.

The End.

THE VERY VERY END

Thus, for Merrily, I had tried to complete the last bit of the story of my life. It seemed such a long time ago, I couldn't remember all of it. So either I left it out or I made it up. But by now I wasn't sure about showing it to Merrily. I didn't think she'd be interested any more since she was no longer held captive by the chickenpox.

To celebrate her recovery, she'd dyed her hair crimson and shaved off one eyebrow. It gave her an odd quizzical look which reminded me of my father wearing his monocle. It might have been acceptable on a raffish playwright in the 1950s. But it didn't look right on my daughter. In fact, it quite upset me seeing my once-lovely child looking so peculiar.

'It's only because it's new and you don't understand the first thing about changing fashion,' Merrily said. Then added gently, 'Because of you being born in a war.'

I thought Harry ought to have a little word with her,

especially about the missing eyebrow. But he wouldn't.

'She's only experimenting,' he said. 'Because she's young. You were young once.'

'Was I? I must be beginning to forget.' Just as well I'd written some of it down.

Merrily found the notebook with the last bit of my life and read it in her usual rapid way, with her normal eye and her naked eyebrow-less eye speeding over the words.

'Well, Mum,' she said, 'it's more or less OK, but you've still left a lot out.'

'How d'you know? You weren't there, except for the very end bit.'

'Yeah, but I've listened to you and Auntie Mary yakking on about the past. You left out about Aunty Mary digging a swimming pool to lure men with. And you left your grandmother out too. You once told me you were named after her. When you were very young, didn't you used to live with her?'

'Yes. I was very ill. She got me better.'

'You ought to write about her too.'

'Very well,' I said. 'Maybe. One day.'

Merrily's brothers, Peregrine, Merlin and Guillemot, came bounding in from playing football in the yard. And her dad, my beloved Harry, came in with a load of logs for the fire. We had crumpets and honey for tea.

Then we all lived and loved happily ever after.

Honest.

Moving Times: Book One

BLOOM OF YOUTH

How was I to know that this rambling country Paradise couldn't last? They say we're in the bloom of youth. Ripe for transformation from uncouth savages to marriageable young ladies. But my sister says that out there is REAL LIFE. Bursting with Passion. Love. Fulfilment. We've got to find it.

For young Ruth the future beckons, rich with dreams. But this is the 1950s. There's no halfway between girlhood and womanhood. So where does a schoolgirl seek Life and Hope before it slips away, beyond reach?

Moving Times: Book Two

GRANDMOTHER'S FOOTSTEPS

I do so much want to follow in her footsteps. On the day the war ended, Granny told me to stick by her and I'd be all right. I'm trying to do just that, to stay as close to her as I can, for ever and ever.

But Ruth's mother, returning from the Victory celebrations, has quite other plans for the family's future. So, in the unfamiliar postwar world, begins a succession of wild schemes, changes and upheavals, different homes, new babies, encounters with strangers. And devastating loss and sadness. But ever present, for young Ruth, is the certain echo of her Granny's footsteps.